THROW

THROW

A Novel

BY

Rubén Degollado

THROW
A Novel

Slant
An Imprint of Wipf and Stock Publishers
199 W. 8th Ave., Suite 3
Eugene, OR 97401

www.wipfandstock.com

PAPERBACK ISBN: 978-1-5326-6508-0
HARDCOVER ISBN: 978-1-5326-6507-3
EBOOK ISBN: 978-1-5326-6509-7

Cataloguing-in-Publication data:

Names: Degollado, Rubén, author.

Title: Throw : a novel / Rubén Degollado.

Description: Eugene, OR: Slant, 2019.

Identifiers: ISBN 978-1-5326-6508-0 (paperback). | ISBN 978-1-5326-6507-3 (hardcover). | ISBN 978-1-5326-6509-7 (ebook).

Subjects: LCSH: Young adult fiction. | Texas—Fiction. | American fiction.

Classification: PS3600 T35 2019 (print) | PS3600 (ebook).

Manufactured in the U.S.A.   APRIL 24, 2019

For Susan Eloise

Llorona de negros ojos,
Ya con esta me despido, Llorona.

Weeping Woman of the black eyes,
With this one [verse], I say goodbye, Weeping Woman.

"La Llorona"
—Andrés Henestrosa Morales

ONE

If I'm going to tell you the story of how I lost two people who were closer than blood to me, I have to begin here in Dennett, Texas, during the summer between the sophomore and junior years of my life. This story begins as it ends, with me, Cirilo Izquierdo, waiting for what all of us spend our whole lives waiting for: to not be alone anymore. The time in between the waiting when we get to be with others, to laugh or to cry or sit in silence with someone next to us, always ends and then we wait again. Like a sentence or prayer or a beautiful verse, there is always punctuation, the little endings of the connections to others in the world, forever the pauses where we leave or someone leaves us, and then again the waiting.

It was Saturday and I was on my parents' front porch, waiting for Ángel and Smiley to pick me up to go to La Plaza Mall and then Tommy's Hobbies. Even though it was still morning, it was already hot outside. Summer days like this, the buzz of chicharras was so loud in the trees you could hear them wherever you were, in your house, or even driving in a car. So many mornings I woke up and this was the first sound I heard. I would hear the cicada's song and know it would be hot outside, which it almost always was in the Valley, except when we got a cold front once in a while.

Where I lived was not exactly barrio, nothing like where the brothers Smiley and Ángel lived over on the South Side. Since Pop had taken over our grandfather's business, Izquierdo and Sons Painting and Drywall, he had gotten himself out of La Zavala, the barrio where he used to live in McAllen, the bigger town close to Dennett.

Back in the day, my Pop had been an old school gangster, the captain of a crew called Los Diggers in the Zavala, made up of his brothers and other kids from the neighborhood. Since many of his friends had died or been put in jail, Pop had gotten it together, spending all of his time at the boxing gym and away from the vagos until he met and married Mama and they moved away. He made sure that he, Mama, and I would never have to live anywhere like that, in houses without air-con, little houses like where my Pop grew up, my Papa Tavo and Abuela Guadalupe's over on Ithaca Avenue.

Pop always said that the one thing in life he was happy about was that he hadn't moved us into another poor neighborhood like the South Side, and that I would never be in a gang. He didn't want us to live anywhere like the Zavala or where Ángel and Smiley and my other friends did, where there were tags on all the walls, tagger crews' names in barely readable but skilled and original letters. Driving through their neighborhood, you could also see the messier HCP tags that were made without skill or pride, graffiti that marked the boundary lines, representing the Hispanics Causing Panic, a gang that Ángel and Smiley and some of my other friends were in since junior high. HCPs weren't like the other big gangs you heard about on the West Coast or across the Valley with veteranos running the show, getting the youngsters to deal or commit crimes. It was mainly just a bunch of locos who ran together, who got initiated, mostly getting jumped in by the other HCPs for a full minute, vowing to always be down for the boys no matter what.

Truth was, me, Pop, and Mama didn't live in *any* kind of neighborhood, not even in one of those new air-conditioned subdivisions where no one talks to each other. With our nice house hidden by mesquite trees and too many rooms for just the three of us, out north on Herrera Road with no one living next to us, Pop, Mama, and I were our own barrio. Even though we were a barrio of three, and Pop had tried to keep me away from that life, it still didn't stop me from being an HCP associate, a friend to the kind of kids my Pop had run with as a youngster.

Pop and Mama had also not liked that I had been going around with a girl from the South Side. My ex-girlfriend, Karina Galán, also known as Llorona, lived there with her mom, in a small house without air conditioning, a house with a wooden floor sitting on blocks, one of those kinds that you could move with a trailer. Even though I didn't want to, I started thinking of her. I could see us in that house together, laughing and telling stories to each other, recording songs from the radio, her dancing in front of me, pretending to be Selena, being different from how we were with the others.

I heard Ángel and Smiley coming all the way down Herrera, and then they pulled up in their father's old flare-side Ford work truck. The brothers had plans to trick it out as soon as they could save up more money, doing audio and alarm system jobs with their cousin Fernando who worked out of his garage. Already he and Smiley had put in a good system, since they said this was the most important place to start with any street sweeper. I didn't have the heart to tell them they just needed to start over, that they should just forget about it.

The bass line was thumping real low when they pulled up. I signed for them to turn it down because my parents were still asleep even though it was almost eleven o'clock. Pop and Mama had been out late the night before, drinking since happy hour (I called it not-so-happy hour), probably at the Gaslight or the Toucan Lounge over by the hospital. They were all hung-over, trying to sleep it off in the coolness of the house.

When I'd walked into their room to get a couple of bucks off of Pop's money clip, the silver one with a gold peso on it, I'd seen them. Pop and Mama are not that old, maybe forty-one or forty-two, but seeing them laid-out like that, thrown around the bed, they looked older than they were. In old pictures I've seen of Mama, she has this clean white skin, long black hair, and big eyelashes. When I look at them, I understand how Pop fell in love with her. In these old pictures, I can also see what she saw in my father. In one black and white photo, just after his younger old school gangster days, he is in a boxer's stance, his hair piled high and greased with Tres Flores pomade, his eyes telling you he owned you no matter how you felt about it. The color of my eyes, a mix of green and brown, my ojos borrados I got from her, but this look I had, the squint that always seemed to be there, was all from Pop.

I asked Ángel, "So, where's that chandelier you were going to put inside?" One time we'd seen this old lady driving a Ford Galaxie that had a crystal chandelier in the back window. This old lady had been riding down the road with just her eyes over the steering wheel, that chandelier moving in all these crazy ways. Ever since then we'd see a tricked-out ride and say it was a real piece of junk if it didn't have a chandelier in the back window.

"You know Güero, same old story, not enough money, not enough luck." He and Smiley and the rest of our friends called me Güero and not Cirilo because my skin was lighter than theirs and because of my eyes. My skin I got from Mama too, who had so much Spanish blood she could pass for a gringa until you heard her talk, and then you'd know she was just as Mexican as the rest of us. The only reason I looked Mexican at all was because of Pop and the Izquierdo side of the family, who were all dark and tall. Even though I was tall like the Izquierdos, I always wished I was dark like them too, because I was a shade between Pop and Mama.

I laughed and said, "Hey Smiley, why don't you get in the middle?"

"Come on, I was here first. I *always* get in the middle. Every day, every day in the middle. You all *always* get your way."

"You don't have to cry about it, cry baby. We only get our way because you're so skinny like a stick, and it's easier if you sit in the middle."

"Ay güey," he said. "If *you* sit next to the window, the chotas are going to pull us over and give us a ticket for being so ugly you're causing all kinds of accidents because people won't be able to take their eyes off of it like they can't look away from a car wreck."

Ángel faked laughing, then stopped real quick and said, "That was *stupid*, Smiley."

Smiley said, "Both you all can kiss my brown nalgas. I don't care what you say. *I* got the window this time."

"See, I knew you could do better. You just had to *apply yourself.*" Ángel said. "*Brown nalgas...that* was funny, and it had class too." Smiley gave this satisfied nod and made sure I saw this.

Smiley got out and held out his hand for me to sit inside as if their truck was a limo and he was the chauffeur. He smiled real big and this wasn't the prettiest thing to see because of his teeth, especially with the sun shining right down on him. Smiley had crooked teeth that looked like yellow seashells all pushed together, but he didn't care who saw his teeth. He smiled without covering up, and he always smiled no matter what he or any of us was going through. This was why we all called him Smiley since no one could remember when. We also called him this because his name was Ismael, so it was pretty natural to call him Smiley. Even the teachers at Dennett High School called him that. You couldn't really call him anything else.

Since I didn't want to argue about it anymore, I got in the middle. What Smiley had said about never getting what he wanted had some truth to it. Smiley had always been the smallest and weakest of us, the kind of friend you don't want to leave alone at clubs or football games or in Mexico—any place where vatos are just looking to beat someone down. With his back all bent over and with his teeth, Smiley was an easy target. You could just *bump* him in the mouth and he'd bleed.

His brother Ángel was the complete opposite. He was taller than me, thick in the chest, shoulders, and arms. He didn't have the gangster slouch. His chin was always up high, challenging the world. Ángel was bench-pressing two forty-five pound plates back in junior high, still lifted weights in the Dennett High School weight room, and could now bench double that. The coaches always told him to go out for football, but he never wanted any of it, and I never knew the real reason other than the fact that he didn't like taking orders from anyone. He would lift weights at the same time as the varsity football players, and none of them ever told him anything, even though not just anyone used that weight room. The thing was, no one *ever* messed with Ángel. It wasn't just because he was built like a lineman or one of those Mexican Mafia vatos from prison. Ángel backed up his size and could throw down and mess you up gacho, sometimes lay you out with one punch. I'd seen him do it.

Besides, I knew this for myself because this is how we had become friends, me and Ángel fighting back when we were seventh graders at Dennett Junior High. I knew how hard he could hit.

TWO

WHEN WE DROVE INTO the La Plaza Mall parking lot in McAllen, there was this long line of cars trying to get out, and a long line of cars trying to get in. It was like cruising Tenth Street on Saturday night. Even though we were from Dennett, we knew McAllen had the most money, the nice stores, and the mall. Even if there was barrio on the South Side of McAllen where my grandma lived, this is where the rich people from Mexico came to shop. The fresas with land and titles could cross the border, then drive back with carloads of name brand clothes and perfumes they had bought at Dillard's, crossing freely unlike the poor Mexicans who crossed the river at night, led by coyotes who took advantage of them.

Money made all the difference in the Valley. Even though all of the towns are pushed together, where you can be on one side of the street and be in one town, then cross the street and be in the other, there are differences between them, and then differences within them. Like Pharr was really hood in some parts and you couldn't just drive into some neighborhoods with your windows open and think you were going to be safe, you could also accidentally drive into a trailer park that was full of Winter Texans with money, old gringos that lived in the Valley while their homes up north were snowed in.

Or you could go to Sharyland and see all of the nice houses and the white people from the old families and wonder if you were still in the Valley, or then see a house with all kinds of Mexican Nationals

7

coming and going, and wonder if they made their money from the import/export business that no one asked about.

Dennett was like that too. It had its barrio and then it had places like where I lived. When you thought about it, each town was a little contradiction, a north side and a south side, rich and poor, old and new. They had this in common, but the difference between the towns is that their extremes are more extreme. Even though you could have rich and poor people in the same towns, we all knew that no one had money like McAllen or Sharyland did and no one had barrios like Dennett or Pharr did.

As we waited in line to get into the mall, Smiley, who was still sitting next to the window, pulled this trick he was always doing. He leaned forward to where someone outside of the truck couldn't see him. Smiley had his head down low and he was laughing.

A car full of girls looked at me and Ángel, and started laughing because we were sitting so close together without a space between us. To everybody outside of the truck, because they couldn't see Smiley, it looked like me and Ángel were sitting all lovey-dovey. I started punching Smiley in the ribs, but he wouldn't sit up straight. He just started laughing harder. So then Ángel put his arm around me and I started punching him too. What I didn't know in that moment was that this stupid game we were playing would later be the thing that changed our lives forever.

I had a little money to spend at the mall since I had taken some from Pop. I hardly ever bought anything besides food because Pop would start wondering where I had gotten money from if he saw new things in my room. Pop might start looking at his money clip, see all these new things, and start wondering. If he ever found out, it would definitely not be good. Even though Pop wasn't like one of those fathers who punched their sons or burned them with cigars, he still slapped me if I messed up or didn't show him or Mama respect.

Pop had these sandpaper hands from working on houses so much. I knew this because one time I had talked real ugly to mama, telling her *Quit being a stupid hypocrite,* because she wouldn't leave me alone about skipping classes. She would sleep in until noon whenever she felt like it, and didn't have to work so I thought, *Who is she, bien mantenida, to be talking?* When Pop came home that day, Mama told him what I had said, and he walked over to the kitchen table where I was eating some fideo with carne picada Mama had made for us. I thought he was going to yell at me, but no, he just walked over and slapped me in the face, which *felt* like being punched. All he said in this quiet voice was, *You ever talk to your mother like that again it's going to be worse.*

That's all he needed to say. I just sat there with a fideo noodle hanging out of my mouth, my face stinging, and knew I would never say anything like that to Mama again.

Ángel said, "Órale, let's go to Rave. Brenda and Gladis were supposed to be there today, shopping." I wondered if my ex was going to be there at Rave with them. I wasn't in any kind of mood to see Llorona La Ex-girlfriend. I didn't want to play the usual ghost games where we tried to pretend we didn't exist to each other.

Karina Galán, who everyone called Llorona, the daughter of the Witch Woman Señora Galán had been out of my life for three months now and I was happy about it. La Ex was gacha, the things she had done to me. With all the things she had done, how she had almost killed herself in junior high, how she had taken the name of a ghost, some people would say she was *bien psycha* and should have stayed in Charter Palms where they put the addicts, nervous breakdowns, and attempted suicides. I had thrown down on so many fools for talking like that about her, but what hurt the most was when Ángel or Smiley or anyone in our circle started talking like this about her, even now that we weren't together and despite how we had broken up.

The thing was, they didn't know her like I used to, how we would talk, how she would show me her book of poems and get all nervous and look away while I read one, how she would ask me what I thought about her one day getting one of her poems with the art on the sides of the page published in *Lowrider Arte* magazine. She

was the only one I ever talked to about reading and books and poems, the books I checked out at the library when Ángel and Smiley
weren't around.

All the others knew was the Llorona identity she had adopted.
We had all heard the stories of La Llorona, each of our parents telling us the story to scare us into being obedient, to never sneak out
of the house at night. The version of La Llorona I grew up hearing
from my mother was about a woman living along the Río Grande
who had fallen in love with a soldier. The soldier told her he loved
her as well, but could never marry her because of her two children.
Out of desperation and her desire to marry the soldier, the woman
drowned her children in the river. When she told the soldier what
she had done, how she was now free to marry, he was disgusted with
her, called her a monster and then left the town. She went mad for
what she had done. She had nothing, no children or a lover. In her
madness, wearing the white wedding dress she had bought in an-
ticipation of her marriage, she threw herself into the river, searching
for her murdered children, drowning herself. Because of her sin,
God didn't let her into heaven and cursed her to forever walk along
the river, weeping for what she has done, calling out, "Mis hijos, my
children, where are you?" Each night she does this, never finding her
own children, and satisfies her guilt by taking the children of others,
making them her own. They are never seen again.

This is who Karina had become, a ghost named Llorona who
dragged others down with her, the girl she had once been long for-
gotten. Would I see Llorona's apparition today? I thought as I walked
towards Rave. Would she drag me down with her?

Rave sold the spaghetti strap blouses, the mini skirts, the short
shorts, the bright stomach shirts and the platform shoes all the bien
buenas liked to wear, the ones where they could show off their pretty
feet with the fancy nail polish.

The three of us walked up to Rave with its bright neon lights
and clothes and some of the girls working there smiled at us as they
hung up blouses and folded.

"Smiley's *here*," Brenda said as she came out of the dressing room, over the thumping techno Rave always had playing. Smiley got all red because he had been mad in love with Brenda since he was a seventh grader and she was an eighth grade *woman*. Smiley had always liked the bigger girls, but in Smiley's eyes, Brenda was the queen of them.

Ángel said, "¿Qué onda, Brenda?" Like every dude we had ever seen around Brenda, none of us could take our eyes off of her. Brenda shows a lot of skin, and she had it all in the right places. Brenda's big *all* over, but *good* big, the best kind of big.

She ran up to Smiley, wearing these green short shorts and this top without straps. Brenda went up and put her arm around him, and it always made me laugh how much bigger she was than him.

Smiley got even redder, and because he was so dark, you knew he was *all* embarrassed.

Brenda pulled him in closer and said, "How's my Cositas doing?" She kissed him on the cheek, and because she was wearing these shoes with big heels, she leaned over him to do it. Her name for Smiley was Cositas, which literally meant Little Things. Whenever we wanted to mess with Smiley and how he was mad in love, we called him Cositas. We always joked about how if they ever hooked up together, he would tag on the restroom walls at school: Cositas and La Brenda, Together Forever.

Smiley looked down at his shoes and said, "Good, y tú?"

"You know me, Cositas. This girl's always *fine*."

"You got that right, girl," Smiley said and made this face like a little kid who's thinking about candy.

Brenda said, "Ay Cositas, you're so cute. When we going to hook up?"

"Just say the word, Brenda, and I'm yours."

"Ay Cositas, you're so chulo and sweet, I wouldn't want to ruin you for other women. You'd be with me and any woman after me would just be a cheap replacement."

Smiley looked at her up and down, and said, *"Ay ruin me, por favor, ruin me."*

Brenda touched the tip of his nose, all flirty like she always did.

All of a sudden, these two older vatos came up behind us from nowhere now that Brenda was acting all in love with Smiley. They didn't smile or throw up their chin in greeting.

Ángel and I turned and looked at them, into their eyes. By not looking away, we gave them a challenge they had to respond to. This kind of situation, it can go two ways, and the way we wanted it to go didn't happen as we were about to find out. I wanted them to lift their chins and keep them there, or spread out their arms, telling us *Qué onda,* without saying anything. Then, all of us would have gone outside to throw blows or bullets.

Brenda knew what was about to go down because she got between us and said, "Hey you all, this is my cousin Rey and his friend Eddie. They're from Pharr. This is Ángel." She put a hand on my arm and said, "And this is Cirilo, but we call him Güero." Something changed in Rey's eyes when Brenda introduced me, and he gave half a smile like he was saying, *I* know *you. I know* about *you.* What was up with that? The vato named Eddie gave Smiley an asco look, like he was disgusted about Smiley talking to Brenda. Smiley didn't even notice the mad-dogging because his eyes were all over Brenda. But Smiley was that way anyway, always putting himself in places where he could get messed up and not even think about it, like crossing train tracks without looking both ways.

Rey and Eddie were both shorter than me or Ángel but were almost as big as Ángel in the shoulders. They were probably eighteen or nineteen, maybe even twenty. Now that we knew Rey was cousins with Brenda, we gave our *qué ondas,* the kind of looks where you just raise your chin a little, don't smile at all, and wait for the other to look away first. If I had kept just looking *down* at him, it still could have started us going a couple of rounds. Brenda put her arms through mine and Ángel's, pulled us away from Rey and asked, "So, how do you all like my new clothes?" Eddie didn't seem to like that too much, the way she turned around in circles for us. *Get over the feeling*, I thought.

The question that kept going off in my head like a firecracker was this: where's Llorona? And as if she knew what I was asking, the dressing room door opened and out she walked. Llorona wore a white shirt that showed her tight brown stomach with the HCP tattoo, her belly button ring and these white pants. She had the blue make up tears on the inner corners of her black eyes, the only tears she cried now. Llorona's hair was pulled back, but with two dagger thin horns of hair, cuernitos pointing to her demonia smile, her small lips shaded a brown so dark it was almost black. Her naked throat was so long and pretty, her collarbone so thin and delicate like a bird's. I remembered holding onto Llorona's neck when I used to walk her to all her classes, which always made me tardy. At first she didn't like me to do this because she said it looked like I owned her. What I had said was that I was proud of her, how beautiful she was, but that I could never own her. Llorona would never belong to anyone. How do you own a ghost?

But Rey was the one who was proud of her today, and with the way he was looking at me, it all started to make sense. For a second Llorona gave me this look like she was going to smile and hug and kiss me, as if these months of us being apart had never really happened. This was the way it was with us. Because we had been together since seventh grade, off and on for almost four years, whenever we saw each other now, it always took a second to remember we weren't together anymore. We were habits to each other. As soon as we did remember we weren't together anymore, the ghost game began, where we pretended to see right through each other. I never told Ángel or Smiley, but I always hoped one of us would stop playing the ghost game, that those seconds of forgetting our not going around would go on and on and turn into minutes and hours and longer, that our apparitions would take shape, becoming flesh and blood and bone, our hands reaching out to one another to make sure we were real.

Llorona smiled and I felt something in my chest, down the back of my neck I had not felt in a long time.

But Llorona wasn't looking at me, and she sure wasn't smiling for me.

She was smiling for Rey.

Qué gacha. This was what his looks were all about.

Rey was looking at her with his player smile, the one that says, *I own you.* Rey had no idea who Llorona was, the kinds of things she could do to people. Did he think we called her Llorona for nothing? Would she be named for the ghost-woman who drowned her babies in the Río Grande River if she was just some pichona you could control, some trained little pigeon who would always come back to you?

Llorona was no harmless little pigeon. She was the lechuza, the owl you see just before someone is about to die, the one that haunts you in your dreams and you never want to see in real life because it means you are about to lose someone you love.

"Te gusta?" He was talking about the clothes. "*I* like. Come on, throw those old rags away and let me pay for these new clothes." He pulled out a thick roll, giving everybody a chance to see. I looked at his hands. Tattooed on the knuckles of his left hand was *El Rey.* Family or not, I wanted to take that roll and stick it in his mouth, to make him cry like a vieja. Who'd he think he was? Coming from Pharr, tattooing *the King* on his hand, buying clothes for a Dennett girl, and then looking to throw me a challenge? Who did this guy think he was? I mean we had hood in Dennett, but not like his neighborhood, where you heard all the rumors about the shootings, the drive-bys, the grandmas getting robbed, that security guard at El Centro Mall getting stabbed with a pencil when there was a fight outside the movies.

If he thought he was moving up in the world just because of some ink that said he was made-up royalty, and being with one of our girls, he was crazy. Here I maybe should've thrown it right back. I should've thrown up my chin and arms, told him, *Qué onda,* this way. But I did nothing, because if I showed any emotion, Llorona would win the game we had been playing. Llorona would get me to admit she still mattered to me. I wanted the game to end, but that didn't mean I was going to lose to make it happen. I wasn't playing that. And besides, he wasn't worth my time and effort.

Llorona laughed like the sweet stupid pichona she never was. Why was she playing this game with him? Even in these months we had been apart, she had never tried to make me jealous. The only game she played was the ghost game, where she pretended not to see me, so I knew that wasn't it. Llorona was putting on a pichona play for something else, but I didn't know why. She walked over with Rey to the counter, tiptoeing with her bare feet on the white tiles. They were talking and laughing and Rey kept looking at me to make sure I knew what was up. His eyes said, *El Rey y Llorona y qué, güey? What are you going to do?*

Our other friend Gladis came from the back of Rave where she'd also been trying on clothes and gave us her saludos in Spanish, which was all she really spoke because she'd only been here a few years. Brenda and Llorona had made friends with her right away, protecting her from the other girls in PE, the ones who called her a mojada and asked her for her green card and all that. And this coming from girls just as brown as Gladis, the only difference being they were Mexicans born on *this* side of the border. Llorona and Brenda had jumped some girls one time for talking like that to her and that was all it took. They left Gladis alone after that, even during those days when Llorona and Brenda were suspended for fighting.

Gladis still had this straight, long pretty hair like girls from Mexico wear it, without lots of hairspray and not colored at all. Gladis was pretty the way she was and she didn't need to change, but she was wearing Rave clothes now, a long sleeve blouse with only two buttons, opened wide at the stomach. Brenda's dad had probably given her some money and she was buying Gladis a little something. Like me, Brenda didn't live in the South Side of Dennett and had a father with money. Our pops even knew each other from both being in the construction business.

Brenda said, "Mira no más. Look at you, girl. Mamasota!" Gladis hid her face in her hair. "Ángel, don't you think she looks good?"

"The young lady is beautiful, noble and true. But you Brenda, you're going to get arrested. Just make sure the chotas don't see you walking down 17th Street in McAllen." Brenda just rolled her eyes. All the time Ángel had known Gladis, he had never said anything like this to her, like he said to Brenda. We never would either. She wasn't that kind of girl.

Gladis parted her hair to find my eyes. She glanced towards Llorona and gave me her smile with no teeth, and I knew what she meant. For some reason, Gladis was always checking on me, seeing how I was when it came to Llorona. Her eyes said, *Sorry, I know how you must feel right now, and I'm sorry.*

Gladis was the only one who knew or cared what was happening in me, so if I kept up the show, I would lose nothing. The best thing to do was to continue to ignore it all, come back to the land of the living, adding Rey to the ghost world where Llorona roamed. But the thing about fantasmas is they don't always stay in their world where they should, and they intrude on the land of flesh and blood. The only thing to do now was to act bored and walk away now that Llorona and Rey were on display, so I wouldn't lose and look weak. Ángel and Brenda asked me where I was going, but I didn't turn around. I just walked out and ignored all the voices coming from Llorona's world. Me walking out made her win in some way, but I didn't care. I *had* to go. I wasn't going to fight for her or show her anything else. Llorona didn't deserve one drop of my blood for what she had done to me, even though I could've taken that fool Rey.

THREE

WHEN I GOT OUT of there, it seemed like all the people in the mall, all the snotty kids and their moms were bumping into me and their voices were too loud and I wanted to get out, to go anywhere but here, like I was a hurt animal wanting to go away and die in some dark corner. I probably would've even gone home if I'd been the one driving.

"Oye Güero espérate, wait up, wait for me güey."

It was Smiley's voice. He said, "Where you going?" Who else could it have been but Smiley? Ángel would have never followed me out, unless it had been his idea to leave. This was how Smiley always had my back. His was the only voice that could be heard in both worlds, the living and the dead. When Llorona was around, I slid into her fantasma land, the place where her cold fingers could reach out and drag me down into her waters of death and desolation. Smiley's voice could pull me back, his words like hands reaching down for me, pulling me up, overpowering Llorona's grip, saving me from the fate she wanted for me, a fate I wanted for myself more and more with each passing moment I spent time in her world.

I didn't say anything, but listened to every word he said, welcoming and not welcoming them, as they pulled me back to the world of light and the living.

Smiley said, "Don't be like that. No te aguites. Do you want to go to Spencer's? Maybe Musicland?"

I went, *psh* through my teeth, telling him, *Forget that noise about Spencer's.*

He said, "Then, let's go outside for a while, smoke a cigarette. ¿Está bien?"

Now we were sitting on the curb at the Dillard's entrance, under a palm tree, trying to get shade because the sun was coming down gacho. Smiley had this camouflage Zippo lighter he always played with. He could do tricks with it, snap his fingers to turn it on, run it along his pants to open it, run it back to turn it on. He played with his lighter more than he smoked. I think he smoked just so he could play with his Zippo lighter.

"You should forget about her." He lit two cigarettes and handed me one. I didn't smoke, just at parties, but I really wanted one.

"I know, I know." I said and blew smoke out of my nose.

"Yeah güey, don't you remember all she put you through? How she wouldn't even let you go anywhere with me or Ángel without getting all jealous. She was always jealous or pissed off at you for something. No está bien. Don't you remember?" He was talking about how any time I wanted to spend time away from her, she always gave me the questions, the looks that could last for days, and this is what he wanted me to remember right then, but that is not what came to my mind. I thought of the moment I first met Llorona in seventh grade, back when she was still known as Karina.

I had walked into the cafeteria with Ángel and Smiley who I'd recently started hanging around with and we saw Karina, Brenda, and Gladis talking quietly to each other, looking our way. I was new to the school, not having gone to elementary in Dennett, and didn't know them. Brenda called out across the cafeteria and said, *Hey you, private school kid, you with the colored eyes, venga! Come over here, my friend wants to tell you something!* Some girls from another table turned around and looked at them and Brenda said, *Hey feas, why don't you take a picture? It lasts longer.* All three of them busted out laughing, and I thought it was a bad idea to go over there and maybe look stupid. I looked at Ángel and Smiley then, and they cocked their heads to the side and shrugged their shoulders, telling me it was my call to make.

I walked over to the girls and Karina was laughing, covering her mouth, while Gladis was trying to clean herself up because milk was coming out of her nose. From the flash I'd seen of Karina's teeth, they were crooked, but not like Smiley's. The two incisors on either side of her front teeth were pushed in toward the center, making them look sharp, almost like a vampire's. Brenda said, *My friend Karina wants to know if you'd like to sit with us.* I sat down and looked into her eyes, which were darker than I had ever seen, almost black. Other times, I would have said the right thing, because I had game even in seventh grade, but in that moment, nothing came to my mind. She tilted her head, leaned in close, grabbed my chin and pulled me closer to her, examining my eyes. She then reached out her hand to shake mine, but still didn't say a word. We didn't let go when we were supposed to release, and everyone got quiet. If there was a beginning to our going around, this was it. There was no *Will you be my girlfriend, Circle Yes or No,* notes, no proclamations of my love, no flowers left in her locker. It was this moment, just our hands reaching out for each other and not letting go until it was time to end it.

"Yeah, I remember," I said now. Whenever someone told me how messed up she was, I thought about this moment in the cafeteria, the girl I knew, who was not like Llorona at all. She was the one who wrote poems about love and hope and read them to me in this shaky, little-girl's voice. I was the only one besides Brenda and Gladis who had read her poems.

What most people like Smiley thought of when they saw Llorona was her standing up on the stadium bleachers at Dennett Junior High. She was up there all messed up on *something,* crying and yelling she didn't deserve to live. I saw her leaning out on the wrong side of the hand railing with her arms out wide behind her, her feet hanging off the ledge.

This was a couple of months after we had met, after everyone knew we were together and everyone still called her Karina. The stadium at Dennett Junior High was way up there and everybody was standing around, looking up. Brenda and some other girls cried into each other's hair and they couldn't answer us when we asked them what was wrong with her. They kept telling me to do something, to help her and shook their hands like they were trying to get something sticky off of them. The teachers kept saying, *Go to class, go to class*, and pushed me back as I tried to get to her, while no one else moved or did anything.

Some idiotas in the crowd yelled up to her, *Jump! Jump-up in the air. Wave 'em like you just don't care.* They said this because if she let go, she would come down for sure. Even though she didn't need to, Brenda asked Ángel and me to jump those mensos and you should have seen them after, all cagados whenever they saw any of us.

Coach Sánchez got closer and closer to her, but she moved away from him, like he was going to hurt her. She cried harder and screamed, *I'm going to jump, I'm going to jump!*

Coach Bernál came at her from the other side and Karina didn't see him because she was trying to get away from Coach Sánchez. And then she got quiet, closed her eyes and let go.

Karina started to fall backwards, her arms out wide, but Coach Bernál reached out and caught her by the wrist. He pulled her up and threw her on the safe side like she didn't weigh anything at all. Later as I played it over in my head, I kept remembering how far away Coach Bernál had been from her when she jumped. I kept wondering how he had gotten to her so fast, how it was impossible.

The chotas finally came and all of us, we just stood out there watching them put Karina into the police car. I remember how her head was down and she couldn't look at any of us. I wanted her to see my eyes, to know that we were all glad she hadn't killed herself. Karina needed to know that counted for something. They took her away to Charter Palms where they put her on suicide watch. All her girls went to go see her, taking her flowers and stuffed animals. I went with them, but had nothing to give her, only my love.

I remember walking into Charter Palms, the woman inside the window asking me to sign in, telling me I had to wait a while because there were too many visitors. I sat down and Coach Bernál was there. I wanted to ask him how it was he had reached out to her, but I didn't say anything. I just sat there while he tried to talk to me.

Cirilo, right? But they call you Güero, *right?*

Yeah, that's it.

Coach Sánchez told me about you. He says you play real good B-ball. You ever thought of going out for the team? You're built for it.

I went *pssh*. Basketball didn't mean anything. Football was the only sport anybody cared about. The basketball teams played whole seasons with only two or three people watching, and these were just girlfriends or moms.

No vale, I said.

Anyway, son. He was one of *those* coaches who called his players *son*. He was trying to treat me like I was one of his football players so I would talk to him, so he could be the important male role model in my life for fifteen minutes. *I came here to visit Karina. Were you at school today? Did you see what happened?*

I thought, *I did and I saw how you reached out for her, how you were the big man and all of us* little boys *couldn't do anything.* I said, Yeah I was there.

It was a miracle, let me tell you, that girl wasn't supposed to die today. I don't know how I caught her, but I did. It was incredible.

I said, *Ya'mbre, you did a great job, we all love you. You have made such a difference in our lives. Teacher of the Year. At least you should get a nice coffee mug out of this.*

Coach Bernál interrupted me and said, *No son, that's not what I'm saying. I'm saying that that girl, she's special. You're her friend and you need to take care of her. Tell her that life is good, that it's worth living.*

Brenda and Gladis came out and they were crying, holding each other all dramatic like they'd just lived through a bombing or hurricane. The door buzzed and the lady in the window said it was okay if I went in now. Coach Bernál nodded at me to walk in and I was glad I didn't have to listen to him anymore.

He said, *You can speak words of life or death to her, son, it's up to you.*

What was up with that? My words never killed or saved anyone and never would. They were just words and always would be.

I walked into the cafeteria where they let everyone visit and there were families at tables, talking all quiet. All I could hear were their voices and the juice machine humming. When she saw me, she walked up real fast and held out her hands. She was crying when she said, *Take me with you. I want to go home. I want to go with you.* No wonder Brenda and Gladis had been crying. My girl was *messed* up.

She put her arms around me and looked up. Her mascara made black lines down her face and when she asked me to get her out of there again, her breath smelled sour, like she'd just woken up. She was wearing flea market rejects, this ugly night-shirt with a teddy bear on the front and these sweatpants. Why did they have to take her clothes too?

We sat down at one of the tables and I was still holding her when she said, *I want to go, I don't want to be here, I want to go home, take me home.*

I told her, *Ssh ssh ssh, it's okay.*

Then like I'd told her something mean, she pulled away real quick and said, *Don't tell me that, don't you ever tell me that. Get out of here! Get out, I don't want you here!*

I said, *Karina I was just. . . .* I didn't get to finish what I was saying because she slapped me in the face and kept on slapping. These big dudes with Charter Palms badges clipped to their belts came in and told me I had to leave. They pulled Karina up and told her visiting time was over, that she had to go to her room now.

Leave me alone! Let me go, let me out! She twisted her body and tried to get free from them, but they held her arms real tight.

They were moving her through the other door when she said to me, *I can't believe you hurt me like this. I can't believe you're not helping me, telling me 'ssh' when I just needed you to be nice. I hate you Güero, I hate you.*

Karina had problems none of us could help her with. Right then I was sure of this, but I also knew something else. I would try to help her anyway, and I loved her even more, in ways I could not explain.

Later when I talked to Brenda about her, she said that Karina changed after that. She didn't need to tell me, though. She was cold to me and for a long time, would not even hold hands with me, as if she was pulling away to some place I could not follow. Everyone saw it, how the girl we knew as Karina was slowly going away. She didn't cry for anything like she used to and she started wearing those blue makeup tears on the inside of her eyes, which made her eyes look even blacker. She started drawing ghost faces and skipping school just to smoke cigarettes at Bonham Hill Cemetery and read the tombstones and would take a long walk to go spend time at the caliche pit where the kids had drowned in the bus accident. She had known a lot of them, and had even been best friends with one of the girls.

Because of this, and because of the Llorona tag she started drawing on her binder and papers, people started calling her Llorona. The only tears were the painted ones now. Then she started to get into more fights, jumping any girl who looked at her wrong, or talked bad about her. I knew she was doing it so everyone would forget about her up there on the bleachers, crying and messed up, out of control. But none of them would forget, and they'd never stop asking why she'd wanted to kill herself. I'd asked Llorona why, and she would ignore the question, as if she couldn't hear me. How had she been hurt enough to want to kill herself? And if she did answer, she would only say, *Maybe someday I'll tell you, Güero. Maybe when I'm stronger.* Months later, she would tell me the truth of what had happened to her, but I never told anyone, because it wasn't my story to tell, no matter what she did to me.

Now Smiley said, "Let me tell you, Llorona's no good for you. Into that brujería of her mama's curses, hearing all that talk from spirits and devils, messing around with that Ouija board. You really want that? She's got you messed up with one of her mama's curses on you. I know from experience. Let me tell you one thing about my jefe. After he'd been drinking and he'd had a few, he used to tell us stories about a bruja he went out with before he met my mom."

"This witch he was going out with was like Llorona and her mother. Any man who left her or did her wrong she would make sick, and just like that—" He tried to snap his fingers. He tried again and said, "And just like that."

I snapped my fingers loud and said, "You mean like that?"

"Yeah güey, you got it, así, just like that, the man would *die*. Now do you want that?"

He talked and his eyes were all big, like he was telling me scary stories near a fire. I laughed because I knew one of his stories was coming, because Smiley was making me forget like he always could. His whole face moved when he told stories, every muscle in his face working to make you think of the story he was telling you, and not about what you were going through at the moment.

"Let me tell you one thing: before my dad married my mom, he was all serious with this witch lady from Mexico named Esmer. Esmer de las Something. Esmer de las Pacas, las Parrancas, Esmer de las something like that. Anyway, my jefe and this lady talked about getting married. My pops soon heard from one of my tías about Esmer's hechizos on people and let me tell you, my pops didn't want to be with a witch woman. So what he did was, he told Esmer he didn't want to go around anymore and you know what? Let me tell you, she put an hechizo around him, but not a curse bad enough to kill him, because she loved him so much. That was the kind of mojo my Dad had with the ladies. But in a way güey, what she did to him was worse. Much, much worse than any kind of death. Let me tell you, what happen was, my pops got this chorro that wouldn't go away. Day and night he was in the bathroom, going and going, pooping his brains out hasta que se echó una bota. Así, like you could a hear a boot hitting the water."

He made his face all red and strained-looking. "All he could do was say, 'I'm going to die, I'm going to die,' and buy all the Gatorade he could buy at the Centrál. De verás güey, it was diarrhea from Satan."

"Whatever, Smiley."

He grabbed my arm, "No, no, no, it was The Evil Runs, güey. For reals, true story, I'm not kidding." I was laughing now, forgetting all about Llorona and Rey.

"I'm serious, ése. Let me tell you, my jefe, he almost died from dehydration and frustration from having to sit on the toilet so much. He even lost his job because of it. So then what he did right, was he hired a curandera to do a cleaning on him, and she rubbed the egg over his body and he was all better. The little egg sucked out all the curse from his body like some kind of spiritual vacuum cleaner. Afterward, my jefe was laying there, sweating. He was thinking how nice it would be to go to the restroom like a normal person without having to kick everybody out of the house, because when he was cursed every cagada was like an exorcism. Then the curandera said she wanted to show my jefe something. She broke the huevito and poured out the yolk, which is normally yellow, right. But let me tell you, the yolk looked all black, like tar or something, and it smelled *gacho*, like menudo that had been left outside for three days. The curandera poured the evil yolk into a coffee can, and said all the evil was there in the Folgers. Let me tell you my dad could never eat eggs again. He would just smell eggs cooking, right, and then get real bad asco like he needed to throw up or have the runs and have to go drop water again. Así."

His face went all red again like he was on the toilet. "'Ay Dios mío, I'm dying. Give me peace.' That was my jefe. He always told us stories like that."

I looked at him as he stared off, thinking about his jefe. What was it like to not have your father anymore, to know that he was gone forever? Mine was a drunk and I barely saw him, but at least he was still physically around. The crazy thing was, Smiley and Ángel's dad was more present in their lives than mine was. I knew because in their apartment, their mom had a shrine set up in his memory. There were snapshots of their father when he was an old school pachuco with the black hairnet and the Stacy Adams shoes. *Old* school. When Ángel was born, he straightened out, quit hanging out on the streets, but it didn't matter. The cancer from the cigarettes got him. The way Ángel and Smiley talked about him, he was a good man when he was alive, letting them smoke cigarettes and drink beer with him if their mama wasn't around, playing cards and always talking about the old days when he was in the gangs in McAllen. My father knew who he was back in the day, and said he would fight with knives or tire irons, always fighting dirty. But like I said all his gangster ways changed when he had Ángel and then Smiley. He had taken care of them and was home a lot. It wasn't good or fair that he was dead.

Real quick, because he could see something else starting in my eyes, he said, "Cirilo, it's a true story, carnál, and I tell it to you so you'll forget about her. Ella no vale."

He was probably right. She wasn't worth it. "You think so, huh?"

"No, I *know* so. If I looked like you, I'd have all kinds of girls calling me all the time. I would be the biggest player around."

"Is that right?"

"Yeah, güey."

FOUR

LATER, WHEN I WAS ready, we caught up with Ángel, Monstruo, Bobby, and Rigo at Spencer's. They were flipping through the posters. This club kid cashier kept looking at them like they were going to steal something, as if they were actually going to try and put one of those poster rolls inside their pants or something.

Rigo looked at the cashier and said loud, "¿Qué onda? HCP *love.*" Rigo was as loud as Monstruo and Bobby were quiet. He was the one always throwing the signs, trying to get all the attention any time we went anywhere. I couldn't remember how many fights he had started. Rigo was the one who said he was puro thug life more than he actually was. Basically, he was a wannabe who hadn't officially been jumped in, but not like I was. I associated with HCP, but I wasn't always trying too hard like Rigo, and didn't roll with Ángel and Smiley because I wanted to belong. I was friends with them because of what we had been through together, how they always had my back and how I had theirs. I didn't have their backs because it was expected, or because I claimed HCP with them. The only jumped in members, the only Puro HCPs I rolled with were Ángel, Smiley, Monstruo, and Bobby and they didn't really care that I wasn't official. It's not like we were Vallucos or Mexican Mafia or Sureños 13 or Norteños or any of the other big gangs. If I really thought about it, when it was just us, we never thought of ourselves as a gang. Ángel and the others took on this identity only when we were around others that didn't roll with us. That is when the throwing of the signs happened, when the tattoos started to come out.

I walked up to Monstruo and Bobby and they put out their hands and gave us their usual silent saludos, the lift of the chin, the smile and the old school handshake, with the three different shakes in one. Monstruo and Bobby went with us to Dennett High School too and were in my grade, but I didn't have any classes with them because we had different schedules. They took classes in the Resource.

Ángel said to me, "You all right?" He raised his big single eyebrow, looked me over, patting my shirt, as if he was looking for stab wounds or bruises. Ángel always spoke in a voice low enough so only we could hear, like even our greetings were not meant to be heard by others. "Don't even stress it, carnál. Don't even worry about it, I told you and told you already. Esa chisquiada, she's not worth it." I didn't like when he called her crazy like that.

Monstruo and Bobby flashed their new Tec-9 shaped rings they'd just bought in Reynosa. Every couple of weeks, Monstruo and Bobby came back from Mexico or the Pulga with some new piece of jewelry. A couple of weeks before this, they had bought pendants with the $ symbol, that had thick "gold" chains.

Rigo said, "You fools showing off that fake gold again? You all killed it already."

Ángel said, "Cállate, güey. Better fake gold than being a fake Mexican who can't even speak Spanish. Puro Almond Joy." Rigo just sucked his teeth and didn't say anything. He never said anything to Ángel.

"Don't be popping your gums at me. ¿Oye Almond Joy, te calmas o te calmo?" Rigo just rolled his eyes and looked away, either because he didn't understand or because he knew better. Rigo could talk real loud, and wasn't afraid of anyone else but Ángel, but couldn't back it up with fists and if he did with words, none of it was ever in Spanish. This was why he was Almond Joy, just as brown as anyone on the outside, but white on the inside because he couldn't speak any Spanish. He basically understood and could say a few words, but if he had to order food, talk smack, or talk to someone's grandma, forget it. Rigo was like my opposite because I was white on the outside and brown on the inside, I laughed to myself.

Smiley backed up Monstruo and Bobby and said, "Miralos. Todos bling-blings." They bought the cheap fake gold in the same stores you could buy the fake Rolex watches that had the hour-marks that fell off and rolled around inside the crystal and the second hands that didn't flutter like the real ones did. I could tell a real Rolex from a fake one because Pop had the real thing, two of them even. The gold Monstruo and Bobby wore faded a week after they bought it, which was why they were always buying something new.

Monstruo and Bobby looked at me to see what I thought of their new jewelry.

"De aquellas, güey," I lied. It was cheap, not good quality jewelry at all.

Bobby took off his ring and said, "You like it, huh? I can lend it if you want."

"No, no, you wear it. It looks better on you. You know me. I don't wear jewelry."

"De veras, Güero, I can lend it. You need some gold. All you wear is that rosary, and you don't even wear it outside." He meant my rosary from First Communion, the one I always had on underneath my shirt. They all told me to show it off, that I should at least get one with the right colors, but they didn't get it. I wore it because it reminded me of my mother's brother-in-law, tío Jorge, my Padrino who had died the year before from a heart test gone wrong in the hospital. He and Madrina had given it to me, along with renting me my tuxedo for the pictures. Padrino and Madrina, my uncle and aunt, were good people and always giving of their time and money to me because they never had any boys, just my three girl cousins. When I was little, I always thought they wanted me to be their son, and if my parents ever died, I knew they would treat me like parents should. I always felt guilty when I thought about living with them if my parents both died. I kept meaning to go see my Madrina, as she was alone now, but I hadn't gotten around to it. It was the same way with my grandma, 'Buelita Guadalupe. I hadn't seen her in a long time either and I needed to.

"No, está bien. I'm fine. You wear it."

Rigo said, "I told you it's stupid, fake gold. He doesn't want to wear that. Güero's family has money, and he can afford the real thing." He looked at Ángel and said, "Yeah, I know, fake-no-speaking-Spanish Coconut Mexican, right, but I know good gold when I see it. The Bargain Bazaar wouldn't even sell the cheap caca they wear." Ángel jerked his fist towards Rigo and he jumped back, almost knocking over a rack of key chains. We all had to laugh at that one.

I said, "Gold's gold, güey. Anyway, qué te importa? What's it matter to you?"

Rigo said, "Whatever, fool, I was trying to back you up anyways. All's I'm saying is if they're going to wear it, they should wear the real thing."

Smiley said to Monstruo and Bobby, "You all got *style*. Don't listen to him. He's just a jealous hater. Hey Bobby, why don't you lend it to me."

All of what Rigo said didn't seem to matter to Monstruo and Bobby because they held out their gun-shaped rings and said, "Puro HCP Soljas." They were always saying this, that they were Pure HCP Soldiers.

Ángel turned away to show them his neck, which had an HCP tattoo in black Old English letters, below his left ear. I wasn't into that, but I did know that Monstruo and Bobby would always give me, Smiley, and Ángel backup no matter what. Basically, they'd do anything Ángel said.

Like the one time when Smiley hadn't studied for a pre-algebra test he needed to pass to get credit for the class, he'd told Ángel about it. Ángel then told Monstruo and Bobby to pull the fire alarms and within a few minutes, all of us were outside in the parking lot at Dennett High School. Smiley got an extra day to study, while Bobby and Monstruo got in-school suspension for three days.

Or the other time at a football game in McAllen when these
fools from the Navarro followed me into the restroom to jump me
for my jacket. When I walked in and they followed me in, Bobby
and Monstruo came right in after them. Monstruo made eye contact
with them in the metal mirrors and lifted his chin and kept it there,
telling them ¿*Que onda?* with that look. They took one look at Bobby
with his hand inside his jacket, as if he was hiding something, and
Monstruo with his yellow skin, dark circles under his eyes, and those
arms that were too long for his body, and they didn't want any of
that. They just walked back out.

Monstruo and Bobby would always back me up because I was
tight with Ángel, who was *Puro HCP for Life*. If any of us lived the
crazy life, it was Ángel. As if throwing down on anyone who crossed
him, and throwing signs wasn't enough, he had forever tagged himself with the HCP tattoo on his neck. Whenever the principal Mr.
Scott saw it Ángel told him it stood for Hermelinda Carlota de las
Pacas, his made-up grandmother's name, but Mr. Scott never believed him, even though he was a gringo and most of them didn't
know any better. Mr. Scott must've taken a G.R.E.A.T class or something and knew that HCP stood for Hispanics Causing Panic. Mr.
Scott stopped sending Ángel home for the tattoo because it never
worked. Every time Ángel got suspended, he came to school anyway,
either by sneaking around the buildings and halls all day or just going to classes like normal. So because Mr. Scott got tired of fighting
with him and having security chase him around the school, what he
started doing was making him put band-aids over the tattoo, which
looked even more thug, like he'd gotten messed up in a fight over the
weekend.

Why wasn't I Puro HCP? How come I'd never been initiated
like Ángel and all my other friends who were running around town,
claiming HCP as their identity? Basically, it was because of when
I left private school in elementary and got sent to Dennett Junior
High. I hated that all the montoneros ran around beating down kids
after school, during lunch and PE, six to one, seven to one. Even

though no one did this anymore, I never forgot it, and thought this way of thinking was weakness and showed how afraid you were.

Pop always said if you're going to be tough you got to be able to stand alone. *A montonero is a coward*, he had said. *A real man can stand alone and doesn't need a montón of his friends to back him up.* He had gotten it into his head that I was getting soft at Our Lady of Lourdes, and said I needed to learn about the real world. That's why he sent me to Dennett Junior High in seventh grade. *I don't want you to be a gallina,* he had said. That's also why he taught me how to box in fifth and sixth grade, to get me ready for the real world in junior high because he remembered how it was in his day in Barrio La Zavala in McAllen. But then, Pop said if I ever ran with the wrong crowd, he'd put me into one of those boot camps where they shave your head and yell at you. I already had the shaved head, but it was the yelling at you part I didn't like. Pop was a drunk and I barely saw him, but he knew some things about life and if he made a threat, he came through with it, even if he always contradicted himself.

Ángel looked at us and said "Órale pues, we're leaving this *chafa* store." Ángel said this, looking at the security wannabe club kid at the checkout counter. He wore a white, shiny club T-shirt that was too tight around his stomach. I mean you could see the shape of his belly button through the shirt. What was up with that? Ángel and I just looked at each other and laughed.

On our way out, Ángel looked at the club kid and said, "Ever heard of XL, homes? It's like size large, but bigger. That Extra Medium isn't working for you."

Of course, Rigo had to open his mouth too. "Yeah, stupid!"

Ángel said, "Can one of you tell me why we still roll with this fool?"

He acted like he didn't hear Ángel, which meant maybe Rigo was learning after all.

FIVE

LATER AT THE FOOD court, I could feel the pizza going all the way down to the bottom of my stomach. At the table next to us, this mother was slapping her son on the head because he was blowing bubbles in his soda. His sister smiled about seeing her brother get hit. The little boy blinked his eyes shut tight and smiled as she kept slapping him on the head. We all laughed and Ángel said, "Mira, el future cagapalo of America." Kid was going to be a troublemaker.

Ángel was talking to Rigo, Monstruo, and Bobby about what they were going to do tonight, but I wasn't hearing any of it. I was looking at the pretty preppy girls a few tables away from us in their nice clothes, bright Americanas, smelling sweet, their white teeth laughing, their eyes trying very hard not to meet mine. They looked like rich gringas who went to Sharyland High School, where all the other rich kids went, where I would have gone if Pop had bought a house any further east of where we lived.

Ángel looked over at me and said, "Hey, Güero, you like those gabachas over there?"

"Just looking, güey."

Ángel said, "Watch this," and got up.

"No'mbre, where you going to go?"

"Don't worry, I'm just going to go talk, see what's up, see if I can get some numbers just to say I did."

I said, "Órale, go try your best," just because I wanted to see what Ángel would do.

33

Ángel said, "Oye Rigo, Monstruo, and Bobby, you all stay here. We don't want you scaring them and then them calling security. Okay?"

The way Monstruo smiled it was like he'd said something nice to him. His real name was Reginald, but he hated it because it was an old man gringo name. Because his dad was nowhere to be found the day he was born, his mother had named him after the doctor who delivered him. He liked Monstruo or Monster better, even if it was because of how scary he looked. Ángel turned back around and asked me if I wanted to go with him.

"Vámonos," I said. I was the only one Ángel wanted on missions like this.

I know it's crazy, but sometimes when I walk into a room like a club or a classroom I get a feeling where everything slows down, everybody's watching me because I'm the baddest Mexican who ever lived, and I own the whole room and nobody can stop me. Walking with Ángel, I got this feeling now and those girls looked at us as if they weren't sure if they wanted to walk away or stay and see what would happen. These were the same type of girls Smiley saw in the halls and went, *Psst oye güerita!* to, the same girls who acted like they didn't see us every time.

"¿Qué onda?"

"*Excuse* me?" the blond one said. Her hair was so blond it was almost white. Girl also had a fake and bake tan. I hated that. Why weren't people ever satisfied with the color they were? Like I was one to talk, right, me wishing I was darker like my dad.

Ángel said, "I said 'what's up,' as in how you bien buenas doing?"

"Just sitting here," the second one said, kind of sweet. She had a little more skin on her than the one who was all attitude. Even though she had lost some weight, was wearing a different style of clothes, I suddenly recognized her as Bell, this girl I'd had for art the year before. Bell was a Hispanglo, a half-white, half-Mexican whose real name was Maribel Porter. Her skin was the white kind that could get all golden brown, but not dark, if she spent time in the sun. Since my mother was light-complected and my father was dark, Bell and I almost had the same color of skin, but hers was pinker, especially in the cheeks.

We had talked a lot with each other in art class and always paired up whenever we had a project. I knew she liked me, and I had liked her in a way too. Bell was nice to everyone, and it didn't matter if they were prep, kicker, thug, grifo, or whatever. If she ever saw a kid sitting alone in class when we were supposed to be doing a project, she would go over and ask if they wanted to join us. Back then in the hallways, I didn't make a big deal that I knew her, and pretty much ignored her, not to be stuck-up, but so that Llorona and her girls wouldn't mess with her. Bell had moved to Sharyland second semester and I never saw her after that, but always wondered how she was doing.

The third one just kept looking at the blonde to see what she was doing. She was the leader. I just lifted my eyebrows, gave each of them a little *what's up* look, not too much, not too little, but made sure I smiled at Bell. I was going to let Ángel do the talking, even though that was *my* specialty and I had an in with Bell. Mama once told me that I had the Izquierdo gift like my father, that I knew exactly what to say to women, exactly when they needed to hear it. She had heard me talking to Llorona on the phone late at night and knew.

"So the reason I came over here was to ask you all what you were doing tonight. Me and my friend Güero here are going to have us a little party at the Hilton. We like to do that, rent a room and buy some champagne and go swimming at midnight with pretty girls." Ángel wasn't doing *too* bad on his own, but as it was about to happen, *I* was the one who got the play.

Bell snapped her fingers, pointed at me and said, "You go to Dennett, don't you?"

"Yeah I do. You seen me there?" I said, acting dumb. I sat down next to Bell, so close our knees were touching. Bell didn't move away from me like the other two would have.

"I think I had you for art. Did you have Ms. Fields last year? Yes, yes, you did! I remember! You won that award in class!"

"Yeah, that's right, I did," I said. Bell looked good still even if she was wearing all the preppy clothes like you see in the magazines. I remember thinking that with the way she sometimes wore dark lipstick and nail polish, the way she wore her hair up, this girl wanted to live the life, at least once in a while. Looking back, maybe she did her makeup like that for me, thinking that was what I liked. Bell didn't look like that now. Her new friends wouldn't allow anything like that. She was a born-again prep. I hoped Bell was still the girl that talked to other kids who weren't like her, like she had talked to me, not scared of my shaved head, my baggy pants and the rosary I wore underneath my shirt.

"I'm sorry, I'm so stupid, but I don't remember your name." Me lying was all part of the game. You could meet some of these girls four or five times and *still* act like you never could remember their names. This was the way the preps played it. I knew the rules from when I was at OLL and was good at them.

She looked a little hurt that I didn't remember her name. I had judged her wrong, and she hadn't totally gone to the prep side of thinking. "You don't remember? Bell, as in 'campana.' Why did he call you 'Güero' when I remember your name was Cirilo?" She pronounced Güero like *Where-o*, like gringos did, but had pronounced Cirilo like she learned how to, saying *See-ree-lo*. At least Bell was trying in front of me. And the thing was she had said these Spanish words without sounding sarcastic at all, like some girls who were trying not to be Mexican did and didn't care if her friends looked down on her for it.

"I got the name Güero from my friends. They call me that because of my skin and my eyes, which are lighter than theirs. I'm so sorry I didn't remember your name." Here I looked down and acted shy.

Bell said, "It's okay." To change the subject, she said, "Hey, look up. I want to see your eyes again." Bell touched my chin with one finger and lifted my head. "They *are* lighter. I forgot how different they were." Her fingers smelled sweet and clean.

"They call you Bell, but I remember your full name was Maribel. You have two names too. I always thought Maribel sounded like a song to me." It wasn't the greatest I had ever come up with, but it was enough to make her smile.

"I never thought of it that way."

"I remember you now, how we worked together on our projects. You just look so different now." I didn't want to say, *you look different because you lost weight*, because she might think I was telling her she used to be fat, or that she was only pretty because she had lost weight. She smiled at that and red came into her cheeks.

Now I was back on track. "I remember this one time we were at the sink washing brushes together and you said something about how it took forever to wash the colors down the sink, that the color kept coming from the brushes. I also remember how your face looked, sort of like a smile, but frustrated at the same time."

"I said that? *I* don't even remember saying that. How could you remember something like that?" You could see the red in her cheeks even more.

"I remember things like this when they make an impression on me." She smiled, tucked her hair behind her ears, and looked away.

I wasn't lying about this. I could remember something someone had said years ago, something that should not have really mattered. I could also remember faces and their expressions exactly. I had them in my head, but anytime I tried to draw them, they never came out right. And even though I could remember these things, I could never remember names unless I thought the person was worth remembering. Bell was one of those kinds of people that stayed with me.

I said, "It is so nice to see you again, Maribel. I always wondered about you and kicked myself that we hadn't kept in touch. I'm glad to see you're all right still," I said, meaning that turning prep hadn't changed her. I shook her hand. Bell had soft hands, and she didn't pull away real quick like some girls did, and she didn't just leave her hand out there like some dead fish. She squeezed mine as tightly as I had squeezed hers.

"*Anyway,*" Ángel said. "Like I was saying, Güero and me—by the way my name's Ángel, and that's my real and only name and doesn't even come close to describing who I am—wanted to come over and say what's up, see what you girls were doing tonight. What's *your* names anyway?"

One was Stephanie and the other was Madison. When they said their names it was like they regretted it, like it was the biggest mistake of their lives. I knew I would forget their names as soon as we walked away from them. I would only remember Bell.

"So yeah, we're going to have a party tonight and we were wondering if you girls wanted to come, I don't know, do something different." On the word *different,* Ángel looked away and showed the HCP tattoo on his neck. Ángel believed that every girl, especially the rich gabachas who were bored with their Beamer and Benz boyfriends, wanted a little thug time now and then, a little piece of the crazy life.

These girls though, they weren't having any, except for Bell maybe. But she wasn't even looking at Ángel. The whole time her eyes were on me, and if she went it wouldn't be because she wanted the thug life. She would go because of me, because of the talks we used to have together.

"No, we're going out with our *boy*friends," the head güera said, the one who thought she should be doing all the talking. She looked at her girls for backup and only one even noticed.

Ángel said, "So what are you all doing, going to the movies like always? Maybe get all adventurous and go across the border?"

The third one, who was all brave now that the mera güera was being tough, said, "*You* don't need to know."

Ángel said, "It's all good, it's okay, we'll leave, you don't got to be scared. Your boyfriends don't have to know anything's going on."

"What do you mean 'anything's going on?' There could never be anything 'going on' with you *ése.*" She said *ése* like *essay.* Here was the voice, the one I was glad Bell hadn't started using in front of her friends.

Ángel smiled and blew a kiss at her. He scratched his forehead with his middle finger. "Güerita listen, when you're with your boy-friend tonight, you're going to be seeing my face the whole time, the face of a real man. Let's go, Güero, these gabachas aren't worth it." It wasn't right that he had grouped Bell in with them, because she was different.

Bell was still looking at me. I got up and shook her hand again, said it was nice to see her.

"Maybe I'll see you later," she said. Somehow it sounded like an apology to me.

We walked back to our table, where Monstruo and Bobby were laughing. Ángel gave them this real gacho look. Rigo was laughing the worst, making sure everyone knew it. "Fake Mexican? Better than being a no-digit-getting-told-in-front-of-the-whole-mall-fake-player." He couldn't stop laughing at that one, until Ángel slapped him on the head and said, "Get over the feeling. Te calmes, o te calmo." Rigo calmed down but kept laughing to himself.

Smiley was coming our way, holding a paper bag of gummy bears he'd bought. That dude could eat candy like nobody else. I could tell Ángel was happy to see him, that him coming would change the subject.

"What are you all laughing at?"

Monstruo said, "Your carnál got told by those gabachas over there." At least I think that's what he said. He always talked so quiet that barely anyone could hear.

Ángel said, "Hey you burros, vámonos let's go walking around." Ángel kept looking at the girls' table and his jaw was twitching like it did when he was mad. Besides he always had to keep moving or he would get bored. Me and Smiley and whoever else was around would always follow him even if we were all right where we were sitting.

Just then, Bobby said, "Guacha, one of those gabachas is coming over here." The girls were getting up to go, and Bell was walking towards me.

I looked at her from the side of my eye and never looked at her straight on like I was waiting for her. This was a part of our game. You couldn't act desperate, like you were waiting your whole life for a girl to talk to you.

She had something in her hand and said, "Uh, Cirilo?" Her voice was shaky like she was nervous, not because she was walking up on a group of gangsters, but because she was talking to me, a boy she liked.

"¿Qué onda?"

"I'm sorry about the way Stephanie and Madison were acting. Here. I wanted to give you this so you could call me some time and we could catch up, maybe even come by my house. I have a pool and like to go swimming on days like this." She handed me a *business card*. It had her address and a number for every way I could get a hold of her.

I turned the card over and must have looked surprised because she said, "I know it's corny that I'm carrying a business card like an old lady who sells insurance, but we made them in my business class as a project and I've been carrying them ever since, trying to give them away so I don't feel like I wasted my money."

"No for real, I think it's classy," I said. I put it in my wallet and said thanks, but not like I was all excited or anything.

"That sounds good Maribel, we'll see what happens. Maybe I'll call you sometime. I'd like that." She smiled at being called by her real name and not hearing it pronounced like *Mary-Bell*.

"Okay yeah that's all, I just wanted to come over here and give you that and say I was sorry for how they were acting. Okay? Let you know that not all Sharyland girls are like that. Yeah, that's all I wanted to say. I'll see you all."

She walked off, turned around, put her hair behind her ears again and said, "Oh, and Cirilo? I don't have a boyfriend."

Bobby and Monstruo went *ooh* in these real low voices, like when someone gets disrespected in front of everyone or someone drops their lunch tray in the cafeteria. They were going *ooh* to Ángel.

"Cállate, burros. The only loving you can get is from your grandmas."

Smiley went *ooh* and started laughing real loud. Most of it was fake, I knew, but he was just giving his brother backup. It's what brothers do, give esquina no matter what.

SIX

OUR THING AFTER THE mall was Tommy's Hobbies on Bonham in this shopping center off the Expressway, over by the Centrál Supermarket where we sometimes went when we went skipping school and the Peter Piper Pizza where all the junior high cagaleros like to hang out. We went there because back in the day we used to make model lowriders together all the time. Me and Smiley would also spend hours drawing together, cars or whatever we saw in magazines. We were both pretty good, even though he liked to draw things, and I preferred drawing people, trying to copy their expressions. It was hard, but I liked doing it. We liked to go to Tommy's Hobbies in the later afternoon as he was closing up because all his time wasn't taken up by the old men with all their train questions. Since Pop always had money to give or to take, and Ángel and Smiley never had any, I used to buy us all kinds of Oldies models: Impalas, Galaxies, Chevy trucks, and Bel Airs. With my stack of *Lowrider* magazines at home we'd try and make them look like the ranflas from the pictures. But now that we were getting older we weren't making the models like we used to. We still went to Tommie's Hobbies almost every weekend to look and pretend we were going to make models together, like we did when were junior high youngsters.

The owner Tommy, this veterano from Vietnam, was nice to us even though most people like the club kid at Spencer's always watched us real close whenever we went into stores. Tommy told us that with our shaved heads and the way we carried ourselves, we reminded him of some of the *Hispanics* he knew from Vietnam. He said they were good guys you could trust your life to, that they'd throw themselves on a grenade if you were a brother to them. He once told us that *Hispanics* had won more medals of honor in World War II and Vietnam *per capita* than any other racial group. You never heard things like that coming from gringos or even Mexicans in the Valley.

We went straight to the models section. Along with the remote control planes and cars and trains, Tommy had the best selection of model kits we knew of. We'd been to Ben Franklin, and they didn't have much. Besides, that was an old lady store. All these moms were always in there, going crazy over the plastic flowers and eucalyptus leaves. They held their kids in close when they saw us. This one time we went, the workers in the red aprons followed us around the store, pretending to clean the shelves or price things. We'd only gone that one time and after that we forgot about going back.

There wasn't anything new we liked at Tommy's, just some new planes and military vehicles. Ángel sucked air through his teeth all disappointed even though we wouldn't have bought anything anyway.

Smiley said, "Oye, when are they ever going to make a '69 Impala. It's a lot more prettier than the '63s and the '65s, but you never see them, not even in the low-rider magazines. What's up with that?"

"No sé, I guess they're just not as popular." I had answered this question I don't know how many times.

"Hey uh, Mr. Tommy, you got anything else in the back? Like a '69 Impala for my brother?" Ángel always asked this when we didn't see anything new.

Tommy said, "Come on boys, look around. Does it look like I got any 'back' around here? What you see is what you get."

That was too easy, but Smiley said, "Hey Tommy, we're just kids, you shouldn't be asking us to look at your 'back' dude. Ain't that against the law?"

"Whatever, smart guy. You *vatos* going to buy anything or what?"

Ángel said, "Not from you, not today, you got nothing to buy."

Tommy said, "So then why do you boys come in? Every week I see you, and it ain't like I'm complaining because you boys are all right. It's just that you all don't ever buy. What's the sense in looking if you ain't ever going to buy?"

We didn't know what to say.

"You know what I think? I think you all are just chicken to walk out of here with a model, you know, like you think all your friends are going to think you're acting like a bunch of little kids."

Ángel went *pssh* through his teeth like Tommy didn't know what he was talking about.

"Yeah tough guy, you can go '*pssh*' all you want, but that's what I think. And you know what? You got the whole rest of your lives to be men. If making a model keeps that good kid in you alive, then I think you should do it. Because as long as you all been coming in here you ain't ever stole nothing I know about. You're good *vatos*."

Then like Ángel was going to thank him for all his advice, he said, "Hey Tommy? Don't say 'vato.' It's not for you."

"Whatever you say, smart guy. Just remember what I told you. Hold on to what you got right now, because once you grow up, it's gone."

We turned to leave. "Te guacho, Tommy."

"I'll 'watch' you all later too. You boys take it easy and be safe." Old people were always telling us this: be safe, be careful, watch yourself. Cuídate.

We laughed as we walked out of the store. Tommy was all right. He wasn't afraid of us, and he didn't mind joking around like we did. A lot of the old people we knew, especially the gringos, were always putting on this show like they'd never done anything wrong or talked about how we should live our lives and told us the things we could and couldn't say. When it came from Tommy we didn't mind hearing all that because we knew he respected us. The only other old guy we could talk to like that was Smiley and Ángel's Uncle Benny, but we went to see him for different reasons.

SEVEN

ANYTIME WE WERE GOING to party, we had to stop at the Tortillería, the one over on Herrera Road where everybody bought their beer and tortillas for their pachangas. The Texas Alcoholic Beverage Commission, or ABC, didn't know about it yet even though they'd busted every other store we'd gone to. It was only me and Ángel inside the Tortillería now. Smiley was sitting outside in the truck because even though they never checked us for ID at the Tortillería, Smiley looked like he was still in junior high, little and skinny like he was. We didn't want to push it. Ángel and I were looking into the one glass refrigerator like we had some important decisions to make even though the only thing we had to figure out was long neck or can or quart.

We were paying the old lady who never smiled or looked at our eyes when some dude walked in and grabbed four quarts like he was in a big-time hurry. I didn't look at his face because you don't do that when you're in such a small space with vatos you don't know. Out of the side of my eye, I did see what he was doing though. He pulled out this gold money clip with a fat roll like Pop's, only thicker. He had these tattoos on his hand and I thought maybe there'd be a tattoo rosary or spider webs, but there were five letters beginning on his thumb that spelled out EL REY. Great, I thought, what was he doing here? Rey walked out before us without saying anything even though he had probably seen who we were. It wasn't like we were all feelings or anything. Ángel was now talking to the girl behind the counter

46

who did the bagging, the old lady's daughter probably, practicing his skills even though she wasn't that great looking. Like I said, he was just practicing, maybe trying to make up for the mall earlier.

When we came out the sun was lower in the sky, and this breeze swept the dirt across the parking lot. Smiley was leaning into the window of this white Honda Accord with a big blue H on the hood. It had wide tires and chrome rims. Like I knew she would be, Llorona was in there. Her hair was up all fancy like it was when she was going out, those cuernitos, little diablo horns of hair pointing down into her smile. I could hear her little laugh, saw her cover her mouth like she always did. Llorona looked forward, saw us come up behind El Rey as he went to the driver's side of the Honda. She saw me, I knew, but her eyes didn't show me anything, that she cared I was there or that me being there made her nervous. Llorona was better at pretending I was a fantasma, a walking, breathing ghost. She just threw out her chin saying *¿Qué onda?* to Ángel, but not me. Ángel barely nodded. He always backed me up that way. Besides, he never really liked Llorona when we were going around, saying that she had changed me too much, that I was wrapped around her little finger.

Rey went to the driver's side, got in, and leaned over. He rubbed Llorona's ears with his fingers, those tattoo knuckles scratching across the smooth of her cheek. His eyes were on us like he was all proud of having himself a girl from our clique, like he was taking our women or something. Then he pumped up his system so Smiley couldn't talk to Llorona anymore. He had no respect. Smiley leaned back away from the window and said, "Chale."

Ángel seemed to know I was going to go over to the car because he said something only we could hear, "Calmado, forget about her. No vale madre."

Then like he was saying it in the same sentence, he threw his chin back and said to Smiley, "Hey burro, let's go."

If Smiley had been talking to a different girl he would have said something ugly back to his brother, but he yelled to Llorona, "Te guacho, check you later," even though she couldn't hear him. Smiley walked toward us carrying this little Swiss Army knife he was always showing off, ready to give me backup in case I needed it. In his own way, Smiley was in my corner too, even though that little knife was a joke and he would never use it anyway.

Then as I was heading to sit between Ángel and Smiley, Ángel said real quiet, "What are you doing, güey? Smiley, sit in the middle." Smiley understood and got in. They did that a lot, backed me up in other ways besides using their fists. They weren't going to let Llorona and El Rey see me sitting in the middle like some little punk.

EIGHT

What Ángel had said to those girls about the hotel room was not all a lie. He had a room for the night, but it wasn't at the Hilton. It was over at the Red Carpet Inn by the Expressway in Pharr, almost under the overpass. Since Ángel looked old enough, he had paid for it at the front desk.

We had to keep the music low so the people next door wouldn't call the chotas and they wouldn't come and bust all of us. Smiley's stereo was on the dresser, pumping. I was sitting on the bed. I looked at myself in the mirror by the TV.

We were waiting for the girls, Brenda and Gladis. Brenda had promised that she wouldn't bring Rey or Llorona. They were going to party somewhere in Mexico. That was good as long as I didn't have to see her tonight. The mood I was in I didn't know what I would do if I saw her and Rey together.

Me, Smiley, Ángel, Rigo, Monstruo, and Bobby were the only ones there. It was getting late, and no girls had showed up yet. We were watching Lucha Libre with the sound off on the TV and comparing it to American wrestling. I didn't really care it was on, even though Pop used to take me to the Arena Coliseo in Reynosa to see the Lucha Libre matches on Friday nights. I just wanted some girls to show up so they could bring the place to life like girls do with their laughter and sweet perfume.

I was bored of waiting and waiting so I got out Bell's business card and dialed the numbers on this chafa phone that had a little red bubble-light on it.

Her phone rang and rang and this gringo's voice came on saying all that about wait after the beep.

I said, "Hey Bell, this is just me Cirilo. I was wondering what's up. I'm just here at the hotel, kicking back, wondering what you were doing. Hey you all turn the music down. I'm on the *phone*. You can call me at . . . Hey Ángel what's the number here again?" He told me, so I told her the numbers. "So anyway give me a call when you can." I didn't want to call her other numbers because it'd make me look desperate. Once that happens, forget it. A girl's got to think you got choices, that you're not some poor menso waiting around the phone for them to call.

When they *finally* got there it was Brenda and Gladis and two other girls, Perla and Araceli. These two girls were buenitas who looked so innocent like they'd never been kissed. You could smell them as Smiley opened the door and waved them in, clean hair and all those different perfumes and just a little smell of cigarette smoke.

Brenda had her arm around Araceli, "Now you fools be nice to my baby cousin, especially *you* Ángel. Ya te conozco, güey. My baby cousin goes to the ninth grade campus. This is her friend Perla. You all remember her from junior high, right?" The way she introduced Perla, in this bored voice, she let us all know she didn't really want her there but was only letting her because of Araceli.

"Oyes," Ángel said, "What do you think I am? Araceli, don't believe anything your cousin says. I'm a gentleman in *every* way. Your prima's crazy, girl. Es una? Una? Una. She's a, what do you call them?"

Rigo said, "Pathological liar?"

Ángel said, "Eso, eso, that's it. Yeah, we're trying to get her help for that." Ángel must have been in a good mood because he let Rigo speak.

Brenda said, "Whatever, Ángel. We'll get me help after we pay for electrolysis for your eyebrow. Ever thought of plucking, güey? Looks like a caterpillar died and got stuck to your forehead. Pinche uni-brow from hell."

Ángel held up his hands and was even laughing at that. "That's a good one, girl. You got me, you got me."

Brenda turned to Rigo, "Y tú, Almond Joy? Nobody asked *you*, fool. 'Che metiche Hispanglo from hell. Oh wait, *I'm sorry*. I didn't mean to be rude speaking Spanish in front of you. Pues let me translate for you. 'Che metiche, as in someone who sticks his nose in everybody's business."

"Calm down, Hubba Bubba. I was just helping out a friend with his vocabulary. I don't think you're a liar. Basically, you're a big bubbles no troubles kind of girl, but not a liar."

Smiley said, "Hey Brenda, do you want me to throw down on this fool right now? Because if you want me to, I will. Just tell me when."

"Ay mi Cositas, you're so sweet, but no, he's not worth it. Believe me, someone else *will* sooner or later, and it'll probably be me." She wasn't kidding about that. I'd seen Brenda fight. Even though she was a rich girl, she could probably take Rigo, because like I said before, he lost every fight he had ever been in, and there were a lot. Rigo always picked fights with vatos bigger than him at the Attik or at school during lunch. He always tried to prove himself in front of the others, but all he proved was that he could lose a fight like a champ. The only one he was afraid of was Ángel, not because of the beat-down he could give him, but because he had the power to tell Rigo not to come around anymore.

"Hola, Perla," I said, louder than everyone so I could change the subject. "How you been, girl?" Perla was one of the girls I would still talk to when Llorona and I first started going around, and even though she never jumped her or anything, Llorona always gave her these real gacha looks like she wanted to.

"Been good, Güero. Long time no see, *stranger*. Where *you* been?" She said *stranger* like she had been saying it to me for years.

"You know, been busy."

She said, "Yeah, I know," in a way that made me know she was thinking of Llorona, about how she had taken up all of my time when we were together. There Llorona was again, I thought, floating around us even though she wasn't even here, intruding into the world of the living.

I said, "Oye, Perla and Araceli, you all want something to drink?"

Brenda threw me a look.

"Come on, let me show you." Right then I didn't care how Brenda looked at me.

The girls didn't seem too sure, but they came with me anyway.

I leaned over the tub filled with ice and got two bottles, and Brenda came in and took them from me. She said to Araceli and Perla, "Here, you all can share this one."

She made her eyes little at me, like she couldn't even stand looking at me. She said, "'Che güey, I'm watching you." To change the subject, she said, "Anyway, don't you *Mexicans* got any cups around here? We supposed to drink from the bottle? ¿Qué creen? You all think we're from the rancho or what?"

Some time passed, forty-five minutes or so, and after everybody got over that awkward part of a party where people don't say much to each other, everybody was laughing about this story Smiley was telling, but I wasn't hearing any of it, wasn't even looking at any of their faces. Where was Llorona? What was she doing with Rey? Would Bell call?

"Oye, Gladis, come here." I patted the bed I was sitting on.

She said in Spanish, "*You* come here," but she came to me anyway and sat on the edge of the bed where I was sitting against the headboard.

"¿Y La Llorona? Where is she?"

In Spanish she said, "Where she always is, walking along the river, crying and crying for drowning her babies." Gladis spoke real Mexican from Mexico Spanish, not like the Tex-Mex Pocho Mocho Spanish we used with English and Spanish thrown in together.

"No, you know what I mean," I said in English.

"I know, I know. You really want to know where she is?"

I nodded yes.

"Why? You still love her? I could tell you were jealous today, the way you left Rave. Or worried. You are always thinking about her?"

I looked at her like she didn't know what she was talking about.

"You know, Güero, you are just like all the little children and old people in Michoacán. A lot of them still believe in La Llorona. You ask them and they say they have seen the Weeping Woman, that she takes little children away if they are out at night so she can love them like her own and then drown them. They also say she kills husbands who are out cheating on their wives. Even if you could prove to them she did not exist, they would still believe. You are just like them. You cannot let Llorona go. You will always believe, even if you tell others a different story. You two, you belong together. You want to know where she is at, I will tell you."

"You know what? I don't care. Forget it, I don't want to know." I didn't believe my own voice.

"That's good. Then let me tell you another thing. You know Llorona used to call you her angel? Not too long ago, she said she always felt safe when you held her and you were the only one who ever cared about her. You know you were the only boy who went to visit her at Charter Palms? That meant a lot to her and she felt so bad for the way she treated you because she said when an angel comes you should never hurt him, no matter what you do. She said, 'If I hurt God it is okay because he deserves it for what he has done to me, but an angel only comes for good, and does what he is told, and you should never ever hurt one.'"

Gladis touched my hand as if knowing where Llorona had gone was the most important thing to me, but she was wrong, I tried to convince myself. I tried to tell myself that right then Llorona could be burning in hell for all I cared. But why was it that any time you thought of an ex, it made you hope they were asking around about you? Why did we have to hope they were talking to others about the way it used to be? That they were thinking little thoughts about you no matter what they were doing, who they were with. I hated that she was right.

A couple hours later, Eddie showed up. When Brenda let him in, she made a big show of it, saying, "*Ay,* Eddie's here," and hugging him. He smiled like he thought he was going to get some, but the baboso didn't know that's how Brenda got when she had been partying, all flirty with every guy she saw. I'd seen I don't know how many sonsos think Brenda wanted some, just to be slammed down in front of everyone. One time at Klub X teen night she had told some vato, *Stop trying to kiss me, güey. Somebody give this homeboy a mint because his breath smells like pickles and hot trash.* Brenda was gacha that way.

All the rest of us got quiet and ignored Brenda and Eddie walking in. Our silences said the same thing: *What are you doing here, güey?* We thought this even though we were in his town of Pharr and not Dennett. The party was ours, and he wasn't invited.

Brenda ignored every hint we were throwing at them. "You want something to drink," she said and took him to the bathroom. On the way there, she touched Smiley's nose all flirty. "Ay, Cositas," she said. Anyone else but Brenda, we would've told her to get out. *Ya vete,* we would have said. I always left her alone because Smiley would get aguitado if I messed with her, get all quiet because he felt like he had to tell me something. Anything we said to Brenda, it's like we were saying it to Smiley. It was bad enough already. Smiley was sitting there, not saying anything as he kept his eyes on them the whole time. I looked at him, sort of shook my head, telling him if he was going to be jealous, to hide it better. He just made his eyes little and looked away.

They came back and Eddie sat down on the dresser and said, "What're you all watching?"

Rigo said, "What's it look like? *Sabado Gigante?* Lucha Libre, fool. Hello, look at the ring, the wrestlers. Grab a clue, güey." Rigo was a punk and a wannabe, but you could always count on him not to ever back down or keep his mouth shut when he had something smart to say to someone he didn't like. At least he could pronounce some of the words right and *sound* like a Mexican.

"What'd you say to me?"

Without getting up or raising his voice, Ángel whistled through his teeth and said, "He called you 'fool' as in you must be a stupid menso coming here to our private party without being invited and then asking us a stupid question like that. And even drinking our stuff."

Eddie was smarter than he looked because he said, "'Ta *bien,* 'ta bien. It's all good. I got no problems with you all. Tranquilos. Just making conversation."

Rigo said, "That's what I thought, stupid."

Ángel said, "Shut up, fool."

Sometime later, Brenda was having fun and Perla and Araceli were too, because they were dancing and trying to get me and Ángel and the others to dance too. Monstruo and Bobby sat there, smiling and shaking their heads no. Rigo was being all loud, making gritos, and we kept having to say, *Shut up, fool,* so he wouldn't get us kicked out. Someone was always telling Rigo to shut up. Monstruo and Bobby sat there smiling, watching the girls dance. At the junior high dances, they'd been the ones sitting on the bleachers, watching me and Ángel out there dancing with all the girls they only talked about dancing with. Eddie sat in the same place the whole time, not saying anything, just watching Brenda move across the room.

Then Smiley got up and started dancing all stupid, waving his hands everywhere. The girls laughed and got around him in a circle. Brenda grabbed him by the hips and pulled him in close. Smiley winked at me like the player he was for those couple of minutes. I could see Eddie's blood in his face, his jaw go tight, but he didn't do or say anything. With all of us there, what was he going to say?

Smiley took off one of his shoes and twirled it above him by the shoelace and said, "¡Pues aquí estoy tirando chancla! Don't be jealous I'm dancing so good!"

All the girls laughed and went, "Ooh," at Smiley. He always danced like he was making fun of dancing because he was afraid to try it for real. Smiley thought that the only way he could avoid looking stupid was by looking stupid on purpose. It worked for him.

Then, like me and Ángel had planned it, we stood up. Ángel went with Araceli and I took Perla's hand. Those times I'd talked to Perla in junior high, the way she came out of nowhere to say hi, did the schoolgirl laughing, I always knew she could be my girl if I wanted.

As we danced I held her close, and she didn't move away from me. Perla's scent was flower perfume and shampoo, so different from Llorona's skin, which had its own sweet smell not from perfume or anything else she put on. Somehow, Llorona always smelled a little like she had just come in from outside, the sun or cool night always in her skin, the breeze of the earth in her clothes and hair.

I did not want to think of her now, but there she was, always around.

To make Llorona go away from me, I said, "I like your hair this way, Perla, how it's straight and it comes down over your shoulder." It wasn't a lie. She had just dyed it blond and she'd straightened it, and she had the kind of caramel candy skin that looked good with that kind of hair.

Perla smiled. And Llorona? I was barely thinking of her at all.

Ángel was over there with Araceli, having the same kind of luck, even though he had a whole different style from me that hadn't worked on those gringas at the mall. Ángel's thing was he was the thug, the one who fought and got into trouble all the time, and *this* helped him get girls. He got them by his reputation alone.

Like I said, my style was I knew exactly what to say and just how to say it. Girls like to hear you say nice things, not just *You look beautiful* or *I love your eyes* or other basic things like that. They want specifics, like you're noticing *every* single thing about them, like *Did you know you have the most delicate fingers?* or *I love how your lips are shaped like a bow.* Also, they want to hear you say their name in a soft voice, in a low whisper. You say it like it's the most important word you've ever said, like it's your *amen,* and soon the girl's yours.

I sat down on one of the beds and pulled Perla close so she'd sit on my lap.

"Did you know I always liked you Güero? Way back in the day when I was a little seventh grader. I bet you didn't know that, right?"

I lied and said, "No Perla, I wish I had known. I always thought you were cute, the way you'd kick back with all the girls, watching us eighth graders walking by. I'd think, esa Perlita she's a little beauty, too gorgeous for someone like me. If I had known, I would've dumped who I was with."

She got all red. Perla didn't weigh anything on my lap. I curled Perla's hair behind her ear. I leaned in real close and kissed her cheek. "Perlita, did you know you have the most beautiful neck, so long and pretty?" With that sweet little laugh and the way her skin was leaning into my touch, how she didn't pull away at all, Perla could be my girl if everybody just went away.

Ángel was already on the other bed kissing Araceli, not caring who was watching. Brenda saw and didn't do anything, even though Araceli was her cousin. She just rolled her eyes and sucked her teeth.

Eddie got the same idea because he moved in closer to Brenda where she was sitting on the dresser by the TV, talking low in that voice we use. Ángel was probably thinking that he was glad Eddie was distracting Brenda so that he could put the moves on Araceli. All of the others, Rigo, Bobby, and Monstruo went outside.

Smiley said, "Where you fools going? They'll bust us if we go out there. Stay in the room."

Pobre Smiley, he was trying to stop what was happening with Brenda. Even though Brenda was never his, he could not stand seeing her with anyone else.

I started doing the same with Perla, putting down the moves. I hadn't kissed a girl since Llorona and the feeling was new. You know how it is when you get close to someone new, you get all warm and shaky. She held back and did not enter the kiss like Llorona did. Llorona was the kind of girl who when you kissed her you knew she wasn't thinking about other things, that the kiss was all that mattered, as if she knew her life would not last long and this would probably be her last.

Then I thought, this is the way it's always going to be, me comparing every girl to Llorona for the rest of my life. I'd be like thirty and married, watering the lawn, holding onto the hose, and thinking about Llorona the whole time. *Maldito sea tu nombre*, I said in my head to get rid of Llorona. I cursed her name to make her go away.

"'Che güey, what do you think you're doing?" Brenda stood over Ángel, pulling Araceli off. I guess it bothered her after all, like she wasn't being a good cousin or something, even though she never should have brought her in the first place, not to a party with us there. She should've known better.

Araceli and Brenda stood next to each other. Their bodies were waving together, and Brenda had her finger in Ángel's face like she was about to slap him. Araceli just looked down at the carpet like she was embarrassed but used to this sort of thing happening.

"You knew I didn't want you being a dog and you did it anyway. Araceli's *my* responsibility, güey. Her mother's my mother's cousin and she told me to take care of her, and here you are. Contrólate, *por favor*." She was worse off than I'd thought, with the way her voice sounded, her words all mixing together. Brenda got this way, acting all responsible when she had no place to talk, like if she could do something good, she could forget about all the other things she was doing.

Perla was still on my lap, and we started laughing.

"What are *you* laughing at?" Brenda said. She came to me and started slapping me on the head like that mama at the mall. Each time she hit me I thought about that kid squinting, thinking, *Por favor, when is this going to be over?* I laughed harder at this thought, at the way Brenda sounded like an old lady, at the way Smiley was now trying to pull her off of me. She was stronger than him and he couldn't move her at all. I could tell he was having fun trying though, smiling the whole time, his hands on her hips. I was on the bed with my guard up. Through my fingers I could tell Brenda was crying. What was up with *that*?

Smiley was still pulling at her when Eddie jumped up and pushed Smiley away. Eddie pushed him hard enough to knock him into the wall and onto the dresser.

Ángel was on Eddie before any of us really knew what was happening, before Smiley could even get back up. It took Eddie by surprise. The thing he didn't know about Ángel was that when Ángel fought, he didn't play the games before, the looks, the challenges. If Ángel wanted to go a few rounds, he didn't talk about it. Ángel just started throwing down without a single word, like a barrio dog who attacked without barking, like he was doing now.

They were both on the ground and Ángel had Eddie pinned by his knees, Eddie's neck held with one hand and Ángel hitting him with the other. Eddie was underneath swinging too, but his punches weren't doing anything to Ángel.

Smiley never got up, even as Rigo, Bobby, and Monstruo came in to check on him. He just sat on the floor, staring off into nothing, water pooling in his eyes, leaning against the wall, his hands on his knees.

Smiley didn't do anything either as all of us began kicking Eddie. Eddie was trying to crawl out of the hotel room, and we kept kicking him down, not saying anything the whole time. Then it hit me how quiet we all were, how the only thing you could hear was the heavy sound of shoes on skin and Brenda's high-pitched pleas for us to stop. Also the word *montoneros* came to my mind. *Montoneros* are cowards, never fighting alone. Pop had taught me that a true man fights one-on-one and never needs his friends to back him up, that this was something that only a coward who was too afraid to stand alone would do. My father had said this every time we were in the garage and he was showing me how to box, sharing the skills from his Golden Gloves boxer days. *You stand up for yourself because you are the only one who matters. People will come and go to your corner, but in the end, it is only you who goes down or keeps standing. You throw down or you go down.*

Brenda tried to jump in the middle of us and stop our steady rhythm of patasos.

Brenda said, "Déjalo, *ya*. Stop it, fools," but it seemed like it was more for show.

Eddie gave up trying to get out, and put his hands over his head and we kept kicking. We were going at it still until we heard Smiley behind us.

He said, "Ya párale. That's enough." Smiley didn't need to say it loud, because it was pretty quiet in the room.

Ángel stopped first, and so did the rest of us. We turned to look at Smiley and he was wiping tears from his eyes with the back of his hand.

Ángel said, "You sure, carnál?" I thought maybe Ángel would have a look of disgust at seeing his brother cry, but he didn't show this at all. He looked worried for his brother.

"Yeah, let him go."

If that had been Rigo, Monstruo, Bobby, or even me, Ángel would have kept going until Eddie was out cold, but because it was Smiley, we all stopped. Smiley had been there for all of us at some time or another, had made us feel better by his stories and laughter when we really needed it. Any time he asked us to do something, we did it, no matter what it was. And he never asked us for much. Had it been anyone else, we still would have jumped Eddie, but because it was Smiley we all threw down harder. Smiley had never hurt anyone else, never said anything mean to anybody and always had your back no matter what.

To Brenda, Smiley said, "Get this dude out of here. Make sure he gets home okay."

She tried to help him up, but Eddie threw her hand away and limped out holding his ribs, without looking at any of us in the face. As I heard his car start outside, I got the feeling that we had begun something, that this was not over at all.

I also thought something else: *whatever comes, bring it.*

NINE

ON SUNDAY WE WENT to see who was showing off their cars at Westside Park out on Ware Road off the Expressway. It was sort of like a lowrider car show every Sunday, but nobody won prizes and there wasn't a bikini contest. Ángel, Smiley, and me went in the afternoon during that time when all the church people and viejitos are taking their siestas and some locos are just waking up. Along with the car clubs, the locos from Mission, McAllen, Pharr-San Juan-Alamo, and Dennett all showed up. Everyone knew that we were there to look at the cars and party, but some cagalero was always messing it up, starting problems with rivals. Because of everything that had happened the night before, and because I knew the locos from Pharr, Eddie and Rey's homies, could be there, I had the feeling that something was going to happen, but I didn't know what.

We—Smiley, Ángel, their cousin Fernando, and me—were standing there smoking cigarettes, the smoke curling up our arms and into our eyes. The air was so still the smoke wasn't blowing anywhere. The thump-thump from all the different systems was in our ears, vibrating through our bones. Shiny rides were everywhere. Sunday at Westside Park was wide rims and white walls, gold and silver braided engine hoses, talk about new parts and Old English placards of all the different car clubs in the Valley.

We were all standing by Fernando's mini-truck, a dropped purple Nissan. Fernando was all right, but I sometimes got the feeling he didn't want me around, like he thought I was a wannabe, like the only reason he even talked to me was because I was tight with his primos. Also, I thought maybe it was because he was older or even because he was from McAllen, from Barrio La Paloma. Like always, he was going off about the hydraulics he was going to put in his mini.

"Anyways, my troquita's going to be all tricked out when I get those hydros. The bed's going to be jumping and dropping with a little button."

"But where you getting the money?" Ángel said to us, but loud enough so Fernando could hear, "The other day I saw this menso at the mall trying to buy a Pure Playaz shirt with the Lone Star Card." This was what the state gave you now instead of food stamps.

Fernando went, "That was your *mama's* card I was trying to use."

Ángel said, "You mean your aunt?"

"No, I mean your mama."

Ángel said, "Why you talking about mamas because your mama's knees are so huangos that's where she keeps her bingo money." We all had to laugh at that one. Smiley was laughing the loudest.

"So anyway, before Ángel started making fun of my mama's saggy knees, I was going to say que when my troquita's done I'm going to enter it into one of those shows they got in Corpus sometimes."

All the other rides were there sparkling in the sun, shiny chrome tailpipes, shiny gold plating on grills and wheels, and I thought Fernando, with his mini, didn't have a chance of ever winning something like that, but I didn't say anything.

The locos around the park all stood around laughing, checking out the couple of girls as much as the cars. Here and there a few wannabes threw signs, trying to start some pedo but it seemed like no one wanted any today.

Just as we started to talk about what kind of lowrider was better, a classic, a mini, or a Euro, I saw Llorona pull into the park with Rey and her girls in Rey's Honda. Eddie wasn't with them. There was this ugly long scratch on the passenger door, like someone had used a butcher knife and not just a key.

"Somebody burned that fool," I said, pointing at the scratch with my eyes.

Smiley laughed. "What'd you think I was doing when I was standing next to his car and the stereo was pumping? He shouldn't have interrupted my conversation like that. It was rude."

I punched him in the arm and said, "Te sales, güey."

Smiley could surprise me sometimes, especially with how aguitado he had looked last night, sitting against the wall, not getting back at Eddie for pushing him, just staring off with the wet eyes, not doing anything.

Anybody who saw Llorona out at Westside Park would say she looked like every other loca. She wore the same falling down baggy jeans and white hoodie. If she wasn't wearing her brown lipstick, she penciled in the lines of her lips. Her black hair was up in clips in a bunch on top of her head, her bangs coming down like it did in the two sharp hair sprayed points. She still had those makeup tears painted on the inner corners of her eyes. These two blue drops looked like they were pouring out of her eyes and down her nose.

The way she explained it in a poem once was that way back before the Aztecs were conquered, these women priests used to sacrifice people with stone knives, wailing and weeping the whole time because they did not want to kill, but they *had* to. There was some bad spirit inside making them do it. That same mal espíritu was what had made the original Llorona, the Weeping Woman, drown her children and weep with guilt, wailing for her lost babies along the Río Grande River. Llorona told everyone she herself was like that, always wanting to be good, but killing people in so many ways. And since she didn't cry anymore she showed these blue tears to the world. Karina said *this* was why she was named Llorona, but I knew what she was hiding, the thing that had been done to her, why her name was Llorona, why she had tried to kill herself. The secret I would keep for her until the day I became a real ghost myself.

That güey Rey got down from the Honda and so did everyone else. She had the Llorona sadness and violence in her eyes, not the usual eyes that laughed at the world she was forced to roam in. Brenda got out of the front all smiles and then so did Gladis and Araceli. *Where was Perla?* Llorona *had* to have known about last night. If they all came over to give their saludos, it wasn't going to be pretty. Because of the look I'd seen in Llorona's eyes, I hoped Perla was nowhere around.

They had parked next to this gray Lincoln, a ride that had no right to be out here, having only primer paint and not even close to being tricked out. Since there weren't that many girls out there that day, they were all hurting their necks to get a look. Rey had this big smile on. Llorona looked so small standing with her girls. *Where was Perla?* I hoped Brenda hadn't told Llorona anything about Perla and me messing around last night or about her acting like Araceli's mama, slapping me like she did. I didn't care about me or what Llorona thought. I cared for Perla.

Rey came up behind Llorona and put his hand on her neck. She moved away and gave him this look like he was El Cucuy with two heads, the Mexican boogeyman. *Idiota*, I thought, *you can't act like you own her out here in front of everybody without it coming back on you.* That smile left his face.

I laughed.

Brenda whispered something into Llorona's ear and she turned around. She pretended to look past, but I knew she had seen me. We were playing the ghost game again. I decided not to play and made my eyes small at her, looked right at her. I wanted her to know I didn't have to ignore her, that I could look straight at her and not care at all. Llorona turned away from me again and said something that made Rey smile. He put his arm around her and this time she didn't push him away.

All of a sudden, I felt warm hands go across my eyes. It was time to play back. I could be gacho too.

"Guess who?" I heard a girl say. It could only be one person. Perla.

"Uh, Fidencia?" Even though it wasn't good Perla was there, it felt good because I knew Llorona was over there watching, acting like she wasn't watching. Because Llorona was here, and because I knew how Llorona had always treated any girl who tried to talk to me, the right thing to do here was to push Perla away, to treat her coldly and ignore her. This would keep Perla safe. If Rey hadn't been there, and if Llorona had pushed him away, that is exactly what I would have done. Saving face here was more important than saving Perla. I knew it was messed up even as I was doing it but couldn't stop it.

"No, chulo. Guess again."

"Uh, Hermelinda Arnulfa de la Paca?"

"*No, chulo.* Give up?"

"Yes, I give up." These days Llorona ignored me, but everyone knew she still didn't want any girl getting close to me. Perla was putting herself in a bad way getting close to me, but she knew what she was doing.

Perla didn't look as pretty in the day. The sun brought out her acne scars even though the makeup was thick. The color was too light for her because her neck was darker than her face and her fake blond hair was more orange than anything. Llorona used to say that girls who couldn't put on their makeup right or pick the right shades were like clowns who everybody should laugh at. I always thought to tell Llorona that her mother wore her makeup like that, but I didn't say anything because once you put her in one of her moods, she could be like that for a long time. You couldn't make fun of her mother no matter what you did.

Perla wore these tight white pants and one of those little shirts from Rave. I started to feel kind of bad because I knew Llorona could jump her if she felt like it, and Perla didn't deserve that. Right now she had the mask of La Llorona on, and she could do anything to look mean, even if she wasn't really supposed to care about me. I started to feel bad and pulled away from Perla because po'recita, the poor girl didn't need Llorona jumping her in front of everyone. Llorona didn't fight like other girls, pulling hair and using her nails. She used her ringed fists and she was fast. Perla wouldn't have a chance. Not many girls would, except for Brenda, but they would never fight each other.

Like this one time at Klub X on teen night when Llorona jumped these girls who'd been smiling at me, I'd tried to stop the fight. Real fast before I even knew what was up she was on one of them, punching her in the face with all her sharp rings. A couple of us were pulling her off, and I got hit with one of her elbows. And then we had all run out of there before security even knew what was up, me holding onto my fat lip, thinking I couldn't believe how hard Llorona could hit even though she was so little.

"How come you didn't call me this morning like I asked?"

"I was too crudo, you know how it is."

Truth was, I wasn't hung-over and wouldn't have called her no matter how messed up I was.

"*Anyways*. What are you doing?"

"Pues aquí no más, you know, I've been around for a while. I was too busy this morning to call. Besides you were probably too cruda too." I hoped she got the hint in my voice, the message that I didn't really want to talk to her anymore.

But some girls you could tell them to go to hell to their face and they'd still think you were flirting with them. "Oh, really? Too busy? I wasn't *that* messed up last night. I knew what I was doing." She saw my eyes were away from her. "You know when you were with Llorona a lot of people said you weren't even free to talk to your friends. They say she was so messed up she'd either kill herself or any girl you were talking to. A lot of people are wondering if that's still true. What do you think?"

What was I supposed to say? I'd heard all this before from everyone. Even though Llorona had this sweet face and these sad black eyes, no one could forget what she'd done in junior high or how she got jealous and jumped girls if they even talked to me. Also, how she used to accuse me of cheating on her, seeing things no one else did.

"I say I am free." With this I looked away from her and this time she got the hint.

"You say that, but you don't know what it is to be free. Esa Llorona, she's still got you wrapped and she's over there laughing at you. Mira."

I looked over there by the white Honda and I didn't see Llorona or any of her friends anymore.

"Give me a call sometime when you're *really* free."

"Sure," I said.

Perla walked away and I watched her go.

"Oye, Güero, she's bien buena and you're going to let her go like that?" Smiley said, checking out her walk too.

He was right. But to Smiley, if a ruca had both legs, she was bien buena. This was what *he* said.

"Guacha, isn't that your ex and all her girls walking over to Perla?" Smiley pointed his chin over by the girls' bathrooms. They surrounded Perla like coyotes do around a hurt animal. I thought of walking over there, doing what I could, but Perla knew what was up when she came over to talk to me. Anyway, Araceli was supposed to be her friend, her backup. Except Araceli was with Brenda now, and she'd do anything Brenda said.

"You going to do something?" Smiley said.

"Yeah, I'm going to watch the show." I guess he thought I was going to jump in there and help Perla like I had helped him with Eddie. Smiley knew better because I started walking fast to where they were. I had to stop what was about to happen.

The way all their bodies were moving I knew they were ready to jump her. One thing my Pop always taught me was to watch the way people moved. *The body never lies. If someone's going to hit you, their body's going to show it*. This thing my Pop taught me was true for everyone I'd ever known except for Ángel and Llorona. If she was going to start throwing down she didn't give anything away. I looked around at all the other faces at the park and they were watching them too, the way Llorona's hands didn't move at all, while her girls kept making fists and crossing their arms and moving their feet like they couldn't wait to get it started.

Llorona stood in front of her not saying anything. Perla threw her hands out.

I saw Llorona's mouth move, but I was too far away to hear what she said. Then Llorona moved her chin to tell her girls to move away and they did. Brenda took a little longer to move, looking Perla in the eye, as if she blamed her for how stupid she had looked the night before. Finally, Brenda moved away. I stopped where I was about twenty feet away from them.

Then Perla said, "*That's* what I thought, *marrana*." Calling Brenda a pig was the wrong thing to do.

Of course, this set Brenda off. She turned back around and jumped on Perla. It was all over. Gladis jumped on her too and so did Araceli, even though she wasn't really hitting her hard, just doing it for show. Llorona just stood there watching, with this smile on her face. Then, like they always do, everybody made a big circle around them, laughing and pointing and cheering. I tried to get through the circle to help Perla out, get the girls off of her, but I couldn't get through the wall of people.

Someone close to her felt bad for Perla and started pulling the girls off with them kicking and scratching anyone who got near. These locos pulling them off of Perla could have started an even bigger fight, but they weren't being rough with them, and they weren't playing mete-mano, trying to get a feel where they could. Even though everyone liked to watch a fight they didn't want to get kicked out of the park today. Someone picked Perla up and her hair was like a bird's nest and her face was all scratched, even more messed up than before. I hoped it wouldn't stay that way.

Po'recita, she was crying and screaming and spitting blood, saying she wanted to fight more. It was good that Brenda and Gladis had just scratched her and kicked and punched her around and pulled some of her hair out. They could have done worse. She'd be all right, but she'd never talk to me again. Right then, I knew I should have walked over sooner when I saw them forming around her, and not put it just on her for choosing to talk to me. She shouldn't have come up to me or talked to Brenda the way she did, but that didn't change what was right. If I'd been there, none of it would have happened. One of Perla's friends from the ninth grade campus put her arm around her and led her away from the crowd.

Llorona came out of the crowd and looked my way. With her middle finger, she pointed to her eye and winked at me. She had given Perla el Mal de Ojo, the Evil Eye.

"Perla's dead," Ángel said. "This ain't over. They're not going to stop messing with her all year, and with her Evil Eye, other bad things are going to happen."

Smiley said, "That's messed up too because she's bien buena."

From her mother, Llorona had gotten the Mal de Ojo. Llorona's mother could look at anyone and pass some maldición on to them. When you give someone the Evil Eye it is because of envy. They have something you want and if you look at them you can hurt them or the thing they own. Here it could be me or Perla that could be dead, even though she didn't own me. Supposedly, the only way you could take away the curse of the Evil Eye was to touch the possession or the person you had looked at with envy. This was why when I used to go to Mexico with my mother, old women would touch my closed eyes and say, *His eyes are so beautiful. Let me touch them so he won't go blind.* It scared me until my mother told me they were touching me to protect me. *If they look at your eyes, and don't touch them, you could lose them because they're envious and they could put the Mal de Ojo on you. So don't be scared, chiquito. Your eyes are a different color, different from everyone else's and they think they are beautiful.*

There she was alone, coming towards me, but her girls were coming up from behind through the crowd, their eyebrows all pushed together because they wanted to throw down some more. Llorona never took her black eyes off of me. The Mal de Ojo was on me now. Brenda was also giving me the same kind of looks, but her look had no curse in it.

Llorona and her girls were gachas because sometimes when they were throwing down they used whatever they had in their hands. There was this vago named Rolando who had made up all of these lies about Gladis because she wouldn't give him any play. So in the halls at school, they had stabbed Rolando in the leg with a pencil and broke off the tip. There were so many people standing around in the crowd that Rolando didn't even know who the stabber was. If this was coming for me now that they were done with Perla, I knew exactly who the stabber would be. And as she walked towards me, I didn't move away or tense up. I just looked into her eyes, unable to do anything else. I knew I wouldn't fight her, like the lost child who runs from La Llorona and tries to fight her, but then realizes this is the way it has to be, stops running and lets her drag him down into the water.

TEN

UP CLOSE SHE WAS even prettier than I remembered. Llorona had this deep brown skin that was so smooth without any granitas, any acne anywhere at all. The only makeup she wore was on her eyes and lips. She had these small little ears that stuck out and made her look a lot younger. With how little she was, Llorona looked like she was still an eighth grader. You had to look into her eyes to know she was older.

"Güero," she said, almost in a whisper. It was the first time she had said anything to me in a long time. Her voice was soft like it was when we were alone together, talking about things we could not tell anyone else.

"¿Qué onda?"

"Pues aquí estoy como siempre, aguantando sin tu amor." Brenda and everyone else laughed at this, at Llorona saying she had always been there, barely making it without my love. I didn't want to admit it to myself, but I wanted to reach for her hand and hold it, pull her in close to me.

"What do you want, Llorona?"

To answer, she said, "Cirilo," and brought her hand to my face and touched my check. Just that, her saying the name she only used when we were alone. Llorona's cold touch made my skin come alive, like a ghost had just passed through me, and I felt the goose bumps on the back of my neck. With this, her lifting the curse of the Mal de Ojo from me, she walked away. Llorona did not say anything else other than my name, and did not look at me again. I wanted her to turn around and say something or smile, but this was all.

We were quiet until Ángel said, "Esa Llorona, she scares *me*."

"That's how she is. She scares everybody," I said. My voice sounded far away, as if someone else was speaking. All I could think of was her cold hand on my face.

All around, everyone knew about Llorona and her mother, the witch, La Bruja Galán. They all heard the stories about both of them. The story that got told a lot was about this one time Llorona spent the night at Brenda's when they were in sixth grade, back when she was still called Karina. That night they were playing with the Ouija Board. Both of them had been trying to get the plastic glass to move, asking, *Spirits, are you there? Spirits, are you with us?* They'd been trying and trying until Llorona got the idea to try it on her own without Brenda's help.

How the story goes, the spirits answered *YES* this time when she asked if they were there. Whenever Brenda or anyone told us this story they made sure to say that she wasn't pushing it, that her fingers were barely touching the pointer.

Then Karina asked it a question, the thing Brenda and Karina *had* to know in sixth grade. *Who will I marry?*

Letter after letter the pointer spelled out one word: *Sadness*.

If Llorona really could hear or see spirits like she said she could it was because she got it from her mother, La Señora Galán, who used to be a curandera, a healer, a card and palm reader when she was still with Karina's father. But the real talk was that after her husband left them, La Señora Galán turned into an hechizera, a woman who was paid to make black magic curses against others, and people started calling her La Bruja Galán but never to her face and never in the open. Wives paid her to put curses on their cheating husbands. The mistresses paid her to curse the marriages where their men were trapped. So many people paid La Bruja Galán to make curses that her whole house was filled with evil candles, black and red ones in the shapes of single men and women, and married couples like you see on wedding cakes.

Her mother didn't even have to work a regular job because so many people went to her. You could walk by Llorona and her mother's house and see every single candle glowing in the windows, each flame a curse on someone's life. La Bruja Galán's curses must have worked, which was why people kept going to see her, but she never got the thing she wanted for herself. Day after day she used her Return to Me powder after she took her baths and said her husband's name seven times just like the orange Vuelve a Mi package told her to, but he never came back. Llorona had not seen him in years, but always talked about finding him again some day.

No matter how scary she was, how much she was like her mother, Llorona had just lifted the curse of her Mal de Ojo from me. That had to count for something.

I looked at Rey who was standing near us now. I smiled and it was like a question. *Would she do that for you?* His mouth made the upside-down U, telling me *No me importa. It doesn't matter to me one way or another; I'm getting what I want from her right now.*

But what I hoped he or anyone couldn't see was how Llorona had cursed me in another way. She had made me remember what it was like to be near her, to have her touch me, the feel of her cold hand on my skin. To make me remember what I had lost was a maldición worse than any Evil Eye. I didn't want any of them to know this.

I watched her go, watched her white T-shirt disappear into the crowd. I wanted to call her back, ask her if we could forget about all this, ask her if she could lift the curse of remembering, and bring us to some kind of present time where we could be together. In spite of everything she had done, I wanted this to happen.

ELEVEN

AFTER THE PARK, ÁNGEL and Smiley had gone home to eat dinner with their mother and they dropped me off. I came into the house, and all I could hear was the hum of the refrigerator and the air conditioning kicking on. Since Pop and Mama were both gone, I knew they had probably gone to the nursing home to see my Papa Tavo who had been sent there after having nervous breakdown after nervous breakdown. On Sunday afternoons, if Mama was home and Pop was out, it meant that he had gone to see his mother, my 'Buelita Guadalupe in McAllen, by himself.

Mama and 'Buelita had never gotten along and Mama never went around there anymore. Before I was born, and they weren't married yet, 'Buelita had told Pop that Mama would be expensive and not good for him. She saw right through Mama's ways, how she had never held a steady job, liked expensive things and going out every night. Then, after I was born, it got even worse. When I was a little kid, 'Buelita accused Mama of not taking care of me like she was supposed to. Any time I was able to go to my grandmother's house with Pop, I ate 'Buelita's carne guisada, beans, and tortillas like I hadn't eaten in weeks. *It looks like your mama doesn't feed you. Only a boy whose mama doesn't feed him eats like that. Pobrecito mi'jito,* she had said in her soft, sing-song voice, stroking my forehead and making the sign of the cross as a blessing. Mama said any time she went over the tías were always judging her, giving her the looks that only women can give each other. So really the only time she came around Pop's side of the family, the Izquierdos, was when there was a quinceañera, wedding, or a funeral.

I thought of going to my room to read or to draw, but I had the restlessness, the feeling that I had to keep moving, that I had to find others to talk to or to be around. Ángel and Smiley had gone home to eat, and I wouldn't see them until tomorrow at summer school. Without fail, they were always home Sunday nights. Even if they didn't all eat together, their mom cooked for them every night, and when the brothers weren't home for any reason, she wrapped the food up for them whenever they got home. Sundays eating together were special to her because that was the only day when their father didn't work late, and they all had gotten to eat together. It was a tradition that Ángel and Smiley were sure they kept.

Then, without even thinking about it, I got Bell's business card out of my wallet. Like I said, she had all of her numbers and even her address on it.

This time, I called her private line and waited for her to answer, actually wanting to hear her voice, even if it was her answering machine.

Bell answered right away and said, "Hello," as if it was a question, like she hadn't been expecting anyone to call. I had really expected her not to answer, and all of a sudden felt stupid and didn't know what to say, which was crazy, because I always knew what to say. I mean it was all good for me to run into her, to talk to her at the mall or to see her out and about, both of us standing next to her car, talking about whatever. I could play that like a winner, and in these kinds of situations, the words just came to me, but now they were just not coming.

"Hey, Bell," I said. It was the best I could do.

"Hey, Cirilo," Bell said and her voice was softer than when she had first answered. Now she sounded as if we had just gotten off the phone minutes before, like she was used to me calling.

"I was just thinking about you, wondering what you were doing. Also, I wanted to say I was sorry for how my friend Ángel acted with your friends." I couldn't believe I had said that. I had never apologized for Ángel or any of my friends and didn't want to start, but like I said, I was having a hard time finding words.

"No, like I told you, and I'm glad you called, it was us who were acting like snobs. I know we're preps, but that doesn't mean we should be acting like that."

"What are you doing right now?"

"Are you asking because you want to know or want to know if you can come over?"

"Both," I said.

"I'm not doing much. I was just on the phone earlier, and yes, you can come over. I'll be looking for you and will come outside."

She gave me directions, we said we would see each other in a few, and I grabbed the keys to Pop's work van, which were always hanging on a hook by the door. He had this beat up white van with Izquierdo and Sons Painting and Drywall plastered on the side, and I knew it wouldn't impress any girls. Pop had told me that if I wanted a car, I would have to work and at least pay part of the payment. He had said he wasn't going to be like one of those parents who gave their kids everything without them having to work for at least part of it. Whenever I was ready and had a job, he would give me his old Ford pickup, the one he and my grandfather Papa Tavo had worked on together or buy me one and make sure I made payments on it.

Bell lived near Sharyland High School. When I turned onto Sunset Lane where she lived, there was this covering of trees, actual trees, not just the short ugly mesquite trees like we had around our house. As it was summer, the sun was still out, but it was low in the sky, and the trees blocked the heat, with the shade from them cooling off the street. Every lawn was mowed and I could smell fresh cut grass and hear the sprinklers. The houses were big and looked like ours in our barrio of three, but unlike ours, they were closer together. Doctors and lawyers and businessmen lived here.

I saw a house that fit the description she had given me and I parked the van a few houses down. I walked up her sidewalk and got that feeling like I didn't belong, like Ángel, Smiley, and I had felt at Ben Franklin when all the old ladies and the kids in the red aprons were staring at us. I felt this even though no one was outside. I knew if I wanted to, I could belong in a place like this, that I could wear the right clothes, have the same haircut, drop the Spanish from my vocabulary and even use some of the big words that I knew from all of my reading. I could fit in anywhere I wanted to because I had gone to OLL and my Pop made a good living and I knew the rules. Even though I was something like a brother to Ángel and Smiley, ready to back them no matter what, I knew they could never belong somewhere like this, that we were different this way. They never said anything about it, and I knew they didn't care.

Something in me made me stop. Sometimes, in moments of my life, I can see things, see a future that I am laying out with whatever I do next. I stood there for a second and saw that me walking up to her house, seeing her this way, would pull me away from Ángel and Smiley and the rest of my friends. Maybe I was making too much out of this, but the look in Bell's eyes, the way her hand had stayed in mine for just a second too long, I knew that this could easily be something more. None of my friends would ever belong in Bell's world and she would never belong in theirs. Just as I turned around to walk back to the van, I heard a door open. From behind me, Bell, in her best chola voice, said, "Hey Güero, where you going?"

"Oh so this is the house," I said, and turned around. "I thought maybe I got the house wrong."

She tilted her head and half-smiled, seeing through my line.

I looked past her, into the windows of her house.

"My parents are home, so let's just take a little walk down the street. There's a little field there where we can sit and talk a little bit before it gets dark."

We walked a ways and came to this open field that looked like kids had played soccer here, the way the grass was beaten down and patchy in spots.

"So, did you end up going to the Hilton?" she asked.

"Not really," I said, thinking of last night, Perla on my lap, Smiley sitting on the floor, and Eddie trying to crawl away from us.

"We had a good time listening to some tunes, having a few together, just kicking it. How about you? What did you do?"

"Nothing interesting, Madison and I just drove around for a while in McAllen. We were going to go dancing in Mexico like usual, but Stephanie had gone out with her boyfriend to the movies, and we never go if we can't all go together. Safety in numbers, you know."

"I guess that means you all are in a gang too."

The tips of her ears went red, and she smiled real big. Then she tried to make an S with her two hands, making two C's on top of each other to form an S, fumbling to get it right, trying to look at her hands as if she was standing in front. She gave me her hardest stare and threw her chin up, holding her two handed sign in front of her, a backwards S.

"Puro Sharyland," she said in her best gangster accent.

"You're the first gangster from Sharyland I've ever known," I said.

She laughed and put her hand on my forearm.

"Sharyland represent," I said and she laughed more. Bell didn't cover her mouth when she laughed like Llorona did. Her teeth were clean and white and it was obvious she'd had braces at one point.

"Hey, but seriously, can I ask you a question?"

I said, "Go ahead, but I already know what you're going to ask."

"How do you know what I'm going to say? You remember faces and expressions. Does this also mean you know what people are going to say before they say it?"

"If you read people like I read books, then yes, most of the time you know what people are going to say."

"So, what is my question?"

79

"You were going to ask me why I am friends with Ángel, Smiley and the other gangsters you saw at the mall?"

"Okay so yeah, I was going to ask you that."

"A lot of reasons."

"Okay, so give me one. I want to know. Because you seem so different from them. I mean not in a bad way, just different."

"'Different,' as in more like you?"

"Maybe."

The sun was lower now and was putting an orange glow across the field, across Bell. The sun was through Bell's hair and it was lighter than it looked inside and the heat outside had started to bring the blood to her face, making her look even prettier than the times I had seen her before.

"For one, they are always there for each other, always there for me. If I'm down, I know Smiley will tell me some stupid story to make me laugh or make a scene in a store. If someone wants to hurt me or is talking bad about me, Ángel will make them regret it. Kids I knew at OLL, they only cared about themselves. They had families at home who gave them everything they needed, and so friends were just kids you knew and spent time having fun together. We are more like brothers who need each other."

"Makes sense. And I hope I didn't offend you by asking. It's just something I've been wondering. I don't know if I could trust my life to Madison and Stephanie or any of the others. So, it's more like family then?"

"Yes, and the thought of losing them is something I don't even want to think about." Something was playing out on my face, and a sad look came into her eyes. She didn't know what else to say, as I could see she didn't really understand what I was talking about. She had parents who loved her, gave her everything she needed. I almost had the same in my life, a nice house, money whenever I asked for it, money whenever I didn't ask for it. I had everything except the one thing I had wanted from my parents when I was younger, for them to spend time with me once in a while. Not that I wanted it now, because I understood that the family you had were the ones that were there for you, the ones who had your back no matter what and weren't too busy with their own lives.

"I better start getting back or my dad is going to wonder where I went, but before we go, I want to see if we can see the sunset. I come here sometimes to see it." We looked off to the west of us, but the clouds were low in the sky, looking like what I imagined a mountain range to look like. We could not see the sun setting, only the ribbon of light lining the top of the clouds and the way the light disappeared from the field around us and dimmed our faces.

As we walked back down her street, Bell put her arm through mine, like they did in the old school days, this thing proper girls did instead of holding hands. I looked over at Bell. She was looking down, but I saw the edges of her half-smile.

We stopped in front of her house. This was the moment when your next move will decide where it will go: a handshake, a hug, a kiss. Bell looked away and I could tell she was nervous, and in a way, I was too. Without wanting to, I thought of Llorona, how the only time I saw her nervous was when she read the toughest of her poems, the ones about the cause of her pain. I thought of Perla too, how her voice had sounded when she had tried to sound tough at the park, which seemed like it had happened years ago, even though it was earlier in the day. Bell's nervousness was the good kind, the only kind a teenage girl my age should have.

I leaned over and did something I had never done before. Bell closed her eyes, and I kissed her forehead.

"Bell, Maribel, you are beautiful and even though I don't want this to hurt you, I need to say it. I shouldn't have come here." I couldn't believe what I was saying, how I was going against every-thing that had ever worked for me, how I could read a girl's face and know exactly what combination of words could get me further with her. She brought her lips together and nodded, telling me she knew it too. I didn't need to tell her any more, didn't need her to know that I didn't want her to end up like Perla, that I could love her, that her goodness and eternal half-smile could pull me back to the land of the living and keep me there, that this was a place I was not ready for.

I started to go, and Bell said, "Hey Cirilo, can I tell you something?"

"Sure," I said, hearing the sadness in my own voice.

"The next time someone speaks, you should listen to them. I mean really listen to them, hear their words and don't think about what you think they are going to say next or think about what they mean or study their faces to respond with what you think you want them to hear. This is a gift you have, the way you know things about people, but an even bigger gift is the ability to listen, just listen without pretending to listen, listen without putting yourself into the person's words. It is a gift you give others instead of just keeping it for yourself."

TWELVE

MONDAY MORNING WAS SUMMER school. I peeked in my parent's room to ask for some money for lunch or to take some if Mama was asleep. The smell of beer and cigarettes was in the walls, and I knew they'd been out again the night before, after they had visited Papa Tavo in the nursing home probably. Pop was already gone on a job, because regardless of how hung-over he was, he never missed work. He would go out and boss his crews around on a few hours sleep like it was nothing. Mama was still in bed. I saw her white leg kicked out of the blanket, and she was snoring. Some things you shouldn't see, right?

Mama breathed in real deep and fast like she did when she got scared.

"Is that you, mi'jo?"

"Yeah, Mama." I thought I hadn't made a sound.

She turned her face to me. She looked messed up with the make-up all black around her eyes, and she had more wrinkles around her eyes than I remembered.

"I was dreaming about you right now, well dreaming about your name. I was thinking about my little brother. Did I ever tell you about when he died?"

I got up to go, not even bothering to ask for money, because it would mean I'd have to stay longer than I needed to. She was probably still drunk, and I'd heard this story more times than I could remember, but I remembered what Bell had said. *Just listen.*

"Where are you going?"

"I'm going to summer school with Ángel."

"Are you leaving right now? I mean is he here and you're leaving right now?"

"No Mama, I'm waiting for him."

"Then talk to me for awhile; we don't talk enough, mi'jo."

"Okay, Mama."

"Well, what I wanted to tell you about was when my little brother died. I was dreaming and remembering right now. Did I ever tell you about it?"

"Yes, Mama."

"Oh yeah, I forgot."

She went on anyway. When they were drunk, Pop's thing was he had to go out for menudo, sing old mariachi songs and corridos. Mama, she had to tell sad old stories of the old days when she lived in the border town Hidalgo with her parents and sisters.

"He had real light hair like my great-grandfather Cirilo, that's why we named him that. And I named you after him, after my brother. You knew that though, right?" Her eyes went up to the ceiling as if she was thinking about it, remembering him.

"Go ahead Mama, I don't remember the story too much." Even though I knew this story so well I could actually see myself walking around in it, I let her go on. *Just listen.*

"Amá fell one time, and I think the baby got wrapped around the umbilical cord. She was almost full-term and she delivered him stillborn and she named him Cirilo after her grandfather. You should have seen her stomach, mi'jo. He would have been a big boy, our only brother. Apá had always wanted a boy and he'd finally gotten him, but then we lost him. Anyway, he was a big boy. Amá said he was as big as a watermelon. It was in the summer and me and my sisters, we were out picking something, I don't remember what, and Apá came to get us in the car. Why can't I remember what we were picking? Was it cantaloupe? Anyway, when we got in the back seat there was a little white casket with our brother in it. The cars were so big back then. We brought him home and then we had a—what do you call it—a velorio where they put candles on the casket and watch the dead person overnight and say goodbye. Neighbors and cousins came and brought pan dulce and coffee and it was the first time I ever drank coffee. Did you know that?"

I was trying hard not to finish her sentences for her and the more I focused on her words, something in me started to actually enjoy hearing the sound of her voice, even though it was a sad story about a dead uncle I would never know, and I had heard it many times. *I mean really listen.*

She went on and I put my hand on her arm. "I didn't understand why old people liked it. It tasted so bitter. They kept coming until about three in the morning, drinking coffee and drinking coffee, and then it was just us, me and mother and father and my sisters. I remember not being able to sleep the whole night with my only little brother there in the closed white casket. In the morning they came in the hearse and we buried him and I remember thinking that if I ever had a baby I would name him Cirilo so my little brother could live somehow. I remember thinking that. I told mother and she just started crying. He would have been such a good man, just like you're turning into." Here she stopped and reached for my hand.

"So handsome and strong, my baby boy." Her voice was getting sleepy.

"Mi'jo, do you want me to make you some breakfast, some migas maybe?"

"Yeah, Mama, that'd be good. I'd like that."

"Sí mi'jo, when I get up I'll make you some migas. Sound good?" Migas was what she used to make me when I was little. Mama would cut up squares of corn tortilla and fry them real crispy like I liked them and mix them in with egg. Then put the migas in tortillas she had made herself.

"Just give me a few minutes, okay? Just let me rest a little more. I got one of my headaches. When I get up, I'll make my baby boy some migas. Sound good?"

"Sí, Mama, it sounds real good."

She was already asleep again, and it was time for me to go.

THIRTEEN

GLADIS, ÁNGEL, AND I were stuck there at summer school, taking English again because we had skipped so much the year before. Our sophomore year, we had had English with Miss Morse together after lunch and since we had open-campus we went skipping a lot and didn't come back. Even though Gladis had let us *be a negative influence on her* like the counselors liked to say, she was still a school girl and talked about going to college over in Edinburg so she could learn business.

I was retaking English because Pop and Mama made me, and besides I didn't want to be a *chafamore* again. If I had just gone to class and done the worksheets, I would have passed. It didn't matter that I had memorized poems, read the stories and understood them in ways teachers didn't. School wasn't about what you knew or understood. It was about turning in the work. I was also there because Pop always said if I didn't get the credits I needed year after year, he would make me drop out and work with him. He said that school was my job and as long as I did what I was supposed to at my job, I could keep working there and not have to hang drywall and paint houses. He still wouldn't buy me a car though. *Si no*, he said, *out you go, out into the real world you go with the other losers making minimum wage to feed themselves.*

Ángel was there in summer school with me because no matter how much he talked about hating school, no matter how many times he said a suspension from school was just like a vacation, he liked being there. On days he was suspended, he still tried to come to school. The first time he got suspended was when he got caught with a water-bottle full of Presidente, and he came to school anyway. They sent him to the alternative school for that one, but that only lasted 60 days. That day he was suspended before they sent him away, during passing time he talked to us and walked around like he was supposed to be there, as if they hadn't told him the only time he could come back was for his hearing. Then, during class time, he hid in different parts of the school: the library, the cafeteria, in the theater. One of the security guards, a cool dude we called Rosco, finally caught him and took him to the office. They couldn't get a hold of his mom or his uncle Benny so he ended up staying in the office all day.

After that, and after he came back from the alternative school, the vice principals told the security guards to watch out for him any time he got suspended. That didn't stop Ángel from waking up early and showing up before school started and coming by the campus after it was over. If Rosco asked him what he was doing there, he would say that he needed to give his brother some lunch money. Rosco, being the cool older dude he was, would say okay and let him stay outside. I think maybe he and the other security guards were as afraid of him as the kids were. Ángel told us he did it because he was checking in on us, but I knew why he came. Like me, he hated being alone at home more than anything else, and secretly, I think he liked to pay attention once in a while.

The Miss was going off about how the only way for the story to end was for Romeo and Juliet to both die. It was too early to be listening to this, especially on a summer morning when practically everyone else I knew was asleep. The Miss wouldn't even let us drink Cokes in the class even though she always had her little cup of coffee with her.

"If you look at the line on page 673, left-hand column," the Miss said, waiting for us to open our literature books, which only a few of us did, "where Shakespeare calls them 'star-crossed lovers,' you'll see they were never meant to be happy. You'll see even the stars were against them. Some things are not supposed to happen. They are doomed to miss each other in this moment, a tragedy that can only end one way."

This one kid raised his hand with this look on his face like he had gotten a great idea he wanted to share with the class.

"Yes Gustavo, did you have a question or was there something you wanted to add to our discussion?" she asked, all excited. Teachers get that some time, that sound in their voice that says, *Yes, finally, I've gotten through to you. I've taught you something.*

"Uh Miss, can I go to the restroom?" And this was the way they were usually answered. I almost felt bad for her that time.

Everyone busted out, and the Miss shooed Gustavo away like he was a fly, with the other look on her face teachers get where they're asking themselves why they're in the job at all. I always asked myself this question. Why would a teacher do this to themselves day after day, especially summer school teachers who had to baby-sit cagaleros like us who couldn't get it together during the regular school year? The little money they got couldn't be worth it.

"So, *getting back* to the discussion, although these two kids, Juliet and Romeo could have been the hope of reconciliation for both of their families, they were never meant to be together. This brings us to the theme of fate. Can we shape our own futures or are they preordained?"

She was about to talk again without waiting for an answer when Ángel said, "You know who the real problem was? Pinche Romeo." Ángel said this without raising his hand, which was always a bad way to start a conversation with the Miss. Besides, he had said a bad word even the gringo teachers knew about. She hadn't been our teacher for long, but it was long enough for us to know that not raising your hand was what annoyed her more. "If he hadn't been such a punk, he wouldn't have killed himself for some jaina. So yeah, we make our own futures, especially when we let our feelings for some stupid little girl tell us what to do."

"*Angel*," the Miss said, warning him that she would send him out with a referral if he didn't watch his language. I hated it that she couldn't look past the bad words or her fear and just listen to what he was saying, how he was participating in his own way. Even though he never passed in the homework, if you asked him the questions whenever we were doing group work, he always had the answers. Like me, he just never felt like writing anything down. See, the thing was, if Ángel was paying attention he understood all of what we read even though his opinions were *always* different from the Miss's and the other kids. Sometimes I agreed with the other kids and even the teachers' opinions, but I never told Ángel because then he would go off, calling me a sell-out, a pinche prep, a coconut, brown on the outside, white on the inside, a Hispanglo. Ángel had a list that kept going. It was the same list he used on Rigo.

"For real, though, if he had owned Juliet instead of her owning him, he wouldn't have drank the poison. You know, if he hadn't been whipped he would've just got up and said, 'Oh my baby, too bad thou art dead,' and walked away. And Juliet when she got up she would've went looking for *him*. Y ya, end of story, forget that noise about the star-crossed lovers. Know what I'm saying?"

"That's an *interesting* interpretation, Angel," the Miss said. I could see her fighting her eyes from rolling up to the ceiling, up to those invisible stars that were supposedly mad at a couple of teenagers. Like the stars cared, right? At least it looked like she was just annoyed and wasn't going to send him out of the class.

Some lambiscón who was trying to get extra credit said, "I think Shakespeare was *implying* that some things aren't in the cosmic scheme of things. Some events aren't meant to *transpire*, no matter how much we desire them." What was this fool doing in summer school anyway? Was the fool trying to get ahead? Graduate early? So what? So he could go to college quicker? Get old faster?

It looked like Ángel was going to make the sign for okay, the thumb and the forefinger together in an O, the other three standing straight up, but instead he brought the hole of his fingers to his mouth and made kissing sounds, the sign of someone being a lambiscón, a suck-up.

"*Yes,*" the Miss said, ignoring Ángel, "that *reinforces* what I told you about fate. This is a common theme in Shakespeare, a theme that was echoed by the literary movement known as *naturalism.*" What was she talking about? She had it all wrong. Had she actually seen the play? What play was she reading? I had read it, and re-read it, seen it, and I knew differently. In that final scene, when Romeo comes up on Juliet and thinks that she is dead, I always thought it could go differently this time, and it could have. If Romeo had just waited, just waited one more minute, it would have made all the difference. It was a choice he made, not fate.

The rest of what she said went *whoosh* way over my head until Ángel busted in with, "You know we read all these stories about people dying because of this stupid idea that they can't control what happens. Fate ni que fate. I control what happens in my world. If I get blasted, it's because I left myself open. If I kill myself like some tonto for a girl, then it's because I was whipped, you know? Ese pedo about fate. Olvídate."

For special effects, someone went, "*Yee-ah.*" This made everyone laugh, even Gladis who never said anything in class. She hid her face behind her black hair, but I could tell she was laughing. I just kept my head down and didn't laugh. Since seventh grade, Ángel and I had always done our best not to be disrespectful to teachers, even when they pushed us and disrespected us to try to get us to react so they could kick us out of class. Ángel always shared his opinions, but he never talked back or called them names. He wasn't disrespectful now, and he was only participating in his own way.

The reason we didn't talk back was because of a substitute we'd had in language arts in junior high. We came in that day and saw the sub had a bowl haircut and real chubby cheeks. She talked so quietly you couldn't hear her. Just after she started trying to give us instructions for the day, some kid in the back called her Tweety Bird and the other kids started laughing. For the rest of the class, she tried to get us to do our worksheet but the kids kept making fun of her, throwing paper and gum at her. I laughed along with them, even though I didn't say anything.

When our regular teacher Ms. Hiler came back the next day, she had this serious look on her face, and we thought she was going to start yelling at us for acting like fools. She then told us that our substitute, Ms. Mackenzie, had been found in her apartment, dead from an apparent suicide. After that we did our best to keep our mouths shut when it came to teachers. I mean I know that she had to have had a lot going on other than a bunch of kids being fools, but still, we were the thing that made her make up her mind about it. I wasn't going to have that on me again.

The Miss gave him the look, which meant he had to leave. If that kid hadn't said anything, Ángel probably might not have been kicked out, but the class made her feel all embarrassed and scared like she didn't have control. On the referral she'd probably write that he'd said *a bad word* in class and that she couldn't tolerate that kind of talk even though the real reason was because she was afraid.

Ángel said, "It's all good, it's all good," took a bow and waved his hand, like he was an actor in one of Shakespeare's plays. He looked at the kid who had said *Yee-ah* and pointed at his own eye, telling him to watch himself. Ángel backed out of the classroom and was gone.

The preps in the class gave the Miss this look that said, *Thank you, Mrs. Perez, you made the right choice. Now that* he's *gone, we can learn.* Other kids just rolled their eyes and sucked their teeth.

I wanted to say something to the Miss, but if I got a referral, Pop would mess me up. I would never call her out in front of the others, but I wanted to tell her one-on-one, *Teachers like you are the ones that make us not want to be here.* I wanted to say, *Just because a student says a stupid bad word or says something you don't agree with, that's no reason to kick them out of class. Ya Miss, get over it. You teachers say you teach us about solving problems, but when a student is a problem all you do is send him away.*

Anyway, I didn't say anything because I never really spoke up in class, even if it was for something good. Whenever I had to answer a question in class, my voice always sounded funny to me, like someone else was talking, like it sounds when you hear yourself on a recording and you ask yourself, *Do I really sound like that?* I usually just drew and listened or just drew. In most teachers' classes, if you kept your mouth shut and didn't bother the teacher, you didn't have to really pay attention. All you had to do was turn in your worksheets to pass the class. You could fail every test, but as long as you did the work you would be okay. The Miss and other kids in the class kept talking. I thought of leaving, but Pop would make me start working with him to teach me a lesson, and I didn't want that at all, especially not now in the summer when it was so hot. The last thing I wanted to do was ride around in one of his painting vans and carry around buckets of paint.

Gladis in the desk behind me tapped my shoulder, and handed me a note. Every once in a while, she would tell me some things about Llorona, tell me the things she said about me. Mostly she just tried to get Llorona and me back together like how she'd been talking to me at the Red Carpet Inn, saying all that about me being Llorona's angel, which probably wasn't even true. Gladis just wanted us to end all happy ever after, you know like they do in the movies. She didn't want us to end up like Romeo and Juliet. I was like every other ex-boyfriend in the history of the world. I wanted to know the chisme about my ex, wanted to know if she thought about me, hear all the things she said.

The note said:
You feel bad about Perla?
Circle YES or NO.

I circled *NO* and handed it back to her. If you could tell someone was lying by how they drew a circle, I would have given myself away.

After she finished writing what I thought was going to be a book, she handed the note back to me. Gladis had taken so much time because she was trying to make her handwriting all pretty, like they taught her to do in Mexico, working real hard to get the English right.

It said, *Perla shouldn't have said that about Brenda what do you think?*

I wrote, *I think Llorona still thinks we're together.* I wanted to write, *It was my fault, and I wish it had never happened,* but Gladis would take that too far, read too much into it and think I was in love with Perla or something, and it would be worse for Perla.

I handed the note back.

She wrote, *And that's bad? You belong together two hearts as one forever. Anyway Llorona was mad about you and Perla. I know she didn't want me to say anything about it don't tell her. Okay? Why don't you call her or write a note.*

I wrote, *I don't write her because of what she did. You can tell her that. She knows.*

Cirilo why don't you forget about that already when she was with you was the only time I saw her happy.

Some things you don't forget like your girlfriend grinding up on some punk on the dance floor right in front of you. As I wrote this I felt the old jealousy coming back, that sick feeling in my stomach that made me want to kill. It was the ugliest feeling I'd ever had.

You can cheat with your body and you can cheat with your heart. Her heart never left you. What about that.

Por favor.

Please? She's loved you since junior high. You going to throw that away. If you started talking to her right now it would be just like it used to.

Like it used to be. I believed her for a second and believing brought so much back, a memory I didn't want, the way it used to be, the day I finally found out what had made Llorona want to throw herself off the top of the stadium in junior high. It was freshman year, and Llorona and me were sitting on her couch and her mom had gone away somewhere we didn't know. We were lying on that old stinky couch of hers next to each other. We held up this *Lowrider Arte* magazine together I had brought over, Llorona with one hand holding up the right page, and my hand holding up the other side. Our heads were touching each other, and I kept breathing her in. We had fun trying to flip the pages without dropping the magazine. We were giggling like little elementary schoolers except we hadn't been smoking at all. We were just drinking glass after glass of her favorite powdered iced tea from H-E-B, which Llorona always made really sweet. We turned the page and saw this girl-clown dressed in a tight white T-shirt, striped Zoot Suit pants and suspenders. She had on one of those old-school hats like the pachucos used to wear. On the clown's face was this sad look that made us go quiet all of a sudden.

Llorona said, *That's me, Güero, I'm like that clown.*

Come on, I said, *You know you're happier than that.* I couldn't understand how she could be sad, and I thought it was because of me. Why do we always think someone else's sadness is about us, as if we were the only ones that mattered in the world?

No really I'm not, she said, and kissed me, as if to keep me from saying more. One of the saddest, but sweetest things in the world is kissing a girl when she's crying. You taste the salt in her tears, and it is like you know her like no one else. I kissed her when she was crying and it was one of the only times in my life when I felt like I was doing something good for someone, that I was sharing her pain for a little bit, making it easier for her. Maybe I would never save kids from a burning building or be a hero, but this was something I could do, try to take away someone's pain for a while.

That day when I kissed her, she told me why she was called Llorona.

What is it? Qué pasó?

Nothing.

Something in her voice told me it was worse than usual, worse than other times when *nothing* was wrong, which always meant that something was wrong. I held her face and looked real deep into her black eyes and I saw something I'd never seen: fear. *Baby, you're okay with me. I'm here, and nothing's going to happen to you. Just tell me what's wrong.*

She said, *No puedo.* She couldn't so I just held her and didn't say anything at all. Girls only get quiet when you say, *Tell me what's wrong. Talk to me.* You just have to wait for them.

She turned away from me, but she let me hold her, didn't mind my breath in her hair, breathing in her sweetness, my hands massaging her back, neck, and shoulders.

We lay like this for a while, like twins in a mama's belly, until Llorona said, *That time in junior high when I was up there, I saw you looking up at me. I already loved you and knew you loved me, but I saw your eyes and I knew, I knew you were different than everybody else who wanted me to throw myself down. I knew I could trust you, that those eyes would never hurt me. I even thought that if I let go from the railing that you would fly up and catch me like the angel that you are. This is why I can say what I'm about to say.*

Go ahead, tell me, and I'll never tell anyone. You can trust me. I'd told girls that so many times to get what I wanted, but now I believed what I was saying. Right then, she could trust me with anything.

She started talking again, but this time in Spanish because this language wrapped around her like a blanket. It made what she was about to say a lot easier. *Back then Amá had this boyfriend because she was lonely and Apá was away, gone somewhere only God knew where. I never liked the way this boyfriend looked at me.* She went on to tell me the rest of what happened, how this man had hurt her. With me trying to see his face, who it was who'd hurt her, my blood went like acid.

Llorona still controlled her voice. It wasn't shaky and she wasn't about to cry. It was like she was floating over the story, telling me what she was seeing. *The whole time, he told me,* Ssh, ssh, ssh. *That's all, no other words but* Ssh, *don't say anything. That's why when you told me that at Charter Palms, I lost it on you. I am so sorry I did that. You were my angel, my beautiful angel, and I hurt you. I'm sorry. I'm sorry.*

I was about to put one finger over her lips to tell her it was okay, that she didn't need to apologize anymore, but I thought it better not to, and put my hand on the side of her face. I knew I would never tell her to be quiet again, would never share all of her story, and would protect her from any man who tried to silence her. She told me more of what happened to her, but I promised then to never tell what she had shared with me.

I wanted his name, wanted to know where he lived so I could find him, so me and Ángel could blast him, take him out of this world. I was about to ask her, but I knew she would not say his name, because saying it would make her go deeper into that memory. Llorona needed to live now, in this moment. She would never tell me who this man was.

I'm so sorry, if I knew who it was I'd do what needs to be done.

I know you would, I know, but it is not important anymore. He is dead already in my mind. I never told Amá. I let her use this man like a drug so she could start forgetting about Apá. But just like a drug, it seemed like he only made her more sad and when he left, Amá was worse than before. It is something that happened. Nothing more.

This sadness was still with me, too much a part of me, as I sat there in the Miss's class writing notes to Gladis. Kids in the class started to move around, bringing me back to what was happening now. The bell was about to ring. The Miss yelled over the noise, "Okay class, tomorrow I have a special surprise for you. We're going to watch the *classic* version of *Romeo and Juliet* so make sure you're on time. Okay? Has anyone seen Gustavo? Did he ever come back?"

FOURTEEN

DURING THE SCHOOL YEAR, there were so many kids at Dennett High School that we had to have open lunch. The cafeteria couldn't fit everybody and they couldn't get all the food out to all the kids in time. We could go anywhere we wanted as long as we came back to fifth period, which was why I was in summer school. Open campus to us sometimes meant skip day. It meant hanging around at the Centrál Supermarket, walking around the neighborhood, smoking cigarettes at the old abandoned water pump-house or going somewhere else if we had a car. But most of the time we didn't have a car, so we went to the Economy Food Store near the school on Bonham or Rudy's Tacos and Food. Sometimes we didn't go back to school. Now that we were in summer school, Ángel and I went to the Economy after class every day because it was run by Ángel's uncle Benny, this old-school cholo who'd found Jesus in prison. The Economy had the best breakfast tacos around, papas a la mexicana, papas con huevo, beans and bacon, all the kinds that we liked.

We were looking at magazines even though the owner had made a sign in black magic marker on cardboard that said: NO FREE READING. THIS AINT NO LIBRARY! The store had these kinds of signs up everywhere, IF YOUR COMING FROM THE HIGH SCHOOL YOU HAVE TO BUY SOMETHING THAN YOU HAVE TO LEAVE! Another one said, ONLY 5 HIGH SCHOOL KIDS IN THIS STORE AT ALL TIME LEAVE BACKPACKS OUTSIDE.

And in case the Mexicans didn't get the messages he had them up in Spanish too.

The owner of Economy had all these signs up, but everyone knew they didn't mean anything when Benny was working. He liked all the kids that came into the store, knew them all by name, and had even given each student his own nickname. The only time he kicked kids out was if he saw them throwing signs. He would tell them to come back tomorrow when they could act right, that Jesus owned the streets. No kid I knew had ever stolen anything from the store or had gotten rowdy when Benny was working. All the stealing and other stuff happened off of Benny's shifts.

This mocoso freshman HCP wannabe I couldn't remember the name of came up to us as Ángel and I were looking at magazines and said, "Güero, did you hear about Perla?" Again? I thought, Again? I'd been hearing about it all day, how she got jumped by Llorona on Sunday, but Llorona hadn't even moved a finger. Why did everyone have to remind me of the part I had played in Perla getting beat down?

"*No*," I said, trying to sound all scared and surprised. "What *happened*?"

"Well, I heard she was at the West Side Park and she got stabbed by Brenda and Llorona because you were making out with her."

"Oh no, why did this have to happen? It's *all* my fault." I said, shaking my fist at the ceiling. It was my fault, but who was this fool for me to tell the truth to?

Ángel just laughed and said, "Calm down, Romeo. You're not the actor. Don't forget I'm the one that got the award for acting by getting kicked out of class."

The freshman I couldn't remember the name of just looked at me with the little eyes, but he wasn't about to say anything. He wasn't as stupid as he looked.

"Hey, see you later, uh, güey," I said, hoping he got the hint.

"Oh, there's something else. I heard you better watch your back." He liked saying this, like it was his way of getting back at me.

This time I got serious. "What do you mean?" Ángel was paying attention too.

"I been hearing talk that her boyfriend, what's his name, Rey, is going to jump you all."

The fact that someone else knew it was news to me.

Ángel said, "Sí como no, güey."

"No for real, I heard it. This dude says you were mad-dogging him and not giving Pharr respect, and that you jumped his friend at the Motel 6. He said you all got to pay for that."

Ángel said, "It was the Red Carpet, fool. If you're going to be telling stories at least get the story straight. Anyway, you tell whoever cares he can come for Güero *anytime* he wants. He knows where we're at. Bunch of cry babies."

"HCP love," he said all proud, showing off for Ángel. He threw HCP and said "Te guacho." Benny threw him a look, and the kid knew better and put his hands down.

To him, Ángel said, "Stupid wannabe."

The freshman laughed, as if Ángel were joking with him. I laughed too and went back to reading the *Lowrider* magazine. I didn't worry about it. As long as I didn't go to Pharr looking for trouble I was okay. If that fool Rey and his friend were smart, he would never come around here. Ángel had so much backup, I never worried about anything. Any one of those kids would throw themselves in front of Ángel just so he would acknowledge them or remember their names, even with the way he treated them. Ángel wasn't like other older gangsters who built the middle schoolers and freshman up, gave them love and respect to their faces to recruit them. Ángel once said, *If they want in, that's on them to earn it, and I'm not going to lie to them and talk to them like they're my carnalitos just so they'll run with us. I already got my brothers.*

"Oye, you muchachas got to buy something and leave," Benny said from behind the counter to some little junior high girls who were looking at the girl magazines with the bright smiling gringas on the cover. For emphasis, he pointed at one of the signs and said,

"This ain't no library!" They looked at us looking at magazines, and then back to him. Their eyes were saying, *What's up with that? That's not fair.*

Benny said all mean, "Oye, muchachas, come here. I want to talk to you."

These girls looked at each other scared. Benny could look scary when he wanted to. Even though he had been out of prison for years, he still had the blurred tattoos and the thick chest and arms from lifting all those weights. He still lifted at Power Gym. One time he had let us be his visitors at the gym and I had watched him bench six forty-five plates like they were nothing. I had seen all of the lifters standing around trying to look like they weren't watching Benny and how much he was lifting.

Ángel said, "Guacha," and nodded over to the counter.

"You all like reading those magazines for free?"

"Sorry, we were just looking."

"How about a burrito? I bet you'd like to eat a burrito for free too. Or maybe some chicken fingers and jo-jos." He pronounced jo-jos like ho-hos and the girls had to laugh a little even though they were scared.

One of them said, "I said, 'I'm sorry.' We'll leave."

"No muchachas, I was being serious. You girls want some burritos?" Then he laughed real big and got out these paper sacks and shook them open. Benny said, "You want hot sauce? Got a special going on burritos today. Free-fifty. That sound good to you, Bookworm? And you, School Girl?"

They looked at each other and wrinkled their noses like they weren't sure what was going on. They nodded yes and walked out with the burritos as Benny rang them up and put the dollar and change in the till from his own pocket.

"Jesus loves you all. Qué estén bendecidas, God bless. Come back and see me, Bookworm y School Girl."

That was Benny. If a couple was being all lovey-dovey in the store, or making out just outside the door, he would yell out, *This ain't no prom!* and then ask them to come in and be good or leave. I'd even seen him get a ruler from the school supply aisle and put it between them, telling them to leave room for the Holy Spirit and then laugh about it. If a kid complained about how expensive something was, he would say, *¿Qué crees? This ain't no Bargain Bazaar!* and then give it to him at a discount anyway if the kid could tell him something funny. He would say, *Tell me a joke that makes me laugh and I'll give it to you at a discount.* Kids would think about it, then start to tell him a joke and Benny would interrupt them by asking, *Wait a second. Would you tell Jesus this joke?* If the kid said yes, and went ahead with the joke, they would get a discount and sometimes get things for free if the joke was really funny.

I was surprised the owner hadn't fired him for all of that, because even though Benny kept dollar bills and change in his pocket to pay the register, word still got out that Benny gave stuff for free, even if it was only half true. The only reason he hadn't been fired was because since Benny had been working there, the store hadn't been held up, hadn't been tagged, and no one had gotten into a fight there or had made a Beer Run, where you run into the store, steal a case and run out.

Ángel and Smiley were his favorite nephews, the ones Benny was trying to save from a hard life on the streets, the life Benny had lived, the life his brother, their dad, had lived back in the day. I knew him better than my own tíos. He let Ángel, me, and Smiley have whatever we wanted as long as we told him what we'd taken, and we didn't go too crazy. The magazines we could look at, but not keep. The only ones he wouldn't let us look at were the ones behind the counter. He wouldn't let *anyone* look at them, or even buy them. He didn't like that they were there, but he didn't own the store. Whenever he worked, he turned the shelf that had them around so that no one could see them and that they wouldn't tempt him. Benny said he was freed by *la sangre de Jesús*, and going back to that life would be like being a dog going back to its vomit. You don't forget it when people say things like that.

I would never forget the first time I met Benny. It was back in junior high when me, Smiley, and Ángel were just starting to be good friends. They took me to the Economy Food Store after school one day and said there was someone they wanted me to meet, that he would hook us up with burritos and taquitos that weren't eaten by the end of the day. I walked into the store and saw this big vato with a goatee, a shaved head and tattoos and one of those power lifter bodies with those thick arms, a big chest and a big stomach that was tight like a punching bag.

Smiley said, *This is our tío Benny. He was in the pinta. Now he's the manager.*

Ángel said, *Yeah, he got strong in there. Right, tío?*

Sí mi'jo, I lifted weights while I was in there, but that's a part of the old life, and I've been freed from my bondage.

Smiley said, *Oye, Güero, I dare you to punch him in the stomach as hard as you can.*

I looked at him like, *N'ombre you can forget that noise.*

Ángel said, *No, really, he doesn't mind, do you tío?*

Benny came out from behind the counter and said, *Dale gas, mi'jo. Hit me with your best shot. I can take it.*

I thought about it for a little while, then got into the southpaw boxer stance my Pop had showed me, right leg forward, left leg back with my fists up.

Benny said, *Órale, I got a professional boxer right here in my store. Hasta un lefty!*

I gave him a left cross, putting my weight into it with my back leg. Benny fell back into one of the shelves. Candy bars, Chick-O-Sticks, Lucas cups and tamarindo paletas went flying everywhere like confetti. Benny's body slapped on the ground. His eyelids fluttered like his eyes were doing somersaults in his head, and his leg was twitching.

Ángel said, *A la fregada, I think you killed him, güey.*

Smiley said, *You really did it, Güero, we better get out of here.*

I leaned over Benny and asked him if he was okay, and all three of them started laughing. Benny put his arms straight up in the air like he was a mummy coming back from the dead. I sucked my teeth and wanted to kick Benny, but I knew better than that.

I was rubbing my wrist. It'd bent back because his big panza was all muscle and no fat.

Benny got up and said, *You're strong, mi'jo. Who taught you to hit that hard?*

My dad taught me.

Oh si, was your dad a boxer or what?

Yeah, a Golden Gloves boxer back in the old days.

You really know how to throw, m'ijo.

Benny nodded in a proud way. He could have made me look more stupid by laughing more, but he gave me respect in front of Ángel and Smiley. I never forgot that. Benny understood us. He said it was because he was once a chavalo just like us, and in his head, he still was.

So there we were eating burritos from under the hot lights with lots of taco sauce and looking at the *Lowrider* featured car of the month, a yellow Impala with these Dayton wire-wheels and gold-plated everything. The girl on the cover had this polka dotted bikini to match the car.

"Hey boys, don't look too hard at that pretty lady or your eyes are going to pop out." Benny made his eyes all big. We laughed. *That's where Smiley got that look from.*

Ángel said to me, "You know one of these days, we should buy a car together and trick it out. After we get it all fixed we can send pictures to *Lowrider*. Then maybe it can win Lowrider of the Year. Can you imagine the money? The girls?"

"Just think about hooking up with one of the models. ¡Híjole, imagínate!" I played along with Ángel's dream, but that feeling I sometimes got where I couldn't imagine any of my friends being in my future came back to me. I never told anyone about that, about how sometimes I tried real hard to look forward to the way things would be, me in my twenties and thirties with a family. Every time I thought about it I could never see Ángel or Smiley or anyone I was friends with. I really couldn't see any of my future.

Ángel said, "Hey, let's go see what Smiley's up to. We can't let that fool sleep all day."

As we were walking out, Benny said, "Hey boys, where you going?"

What he was really saying was, *Hey boys, where you going without acknowledging me?* We both stopped and shook Benny's hand across the counter and told him we'd see him later. This is the way it is with us, why it takes a Mexican so long to leave a party. When you arrive anywhere your family is, you have to shake *all* the hands, hug and kiss *all* the ladies, and then when you leave, you have to announce that you're leaving and why, and then repeat the process, never saying *adios,* or *goodbye,* but only, *see you later, hasta luego,* or *nos vemos.* My mother taught me that if you say *goodbye,* then it is almost like you are speaking death over yourself or over the one you are saying *goodbye* to. To me, this always seemed like a contradiction because she and Pop also taught me to hug and kiss everyone on the way out. Because life is short, and you never know what could happen. Anyway, if you try to sneak out without doing that, forget about it.

Benny said, "Oyes, you all be careful."

"Always careful, tío."

"Hey boys, remember what I told you."

"Yes, I know Benny." He was talking about God's love for us, how we are supposed to treat others and to stay away from drugs.

He said it any way. "Órale pues, you all be good, Jesus loves you, don't smoke weed, don't drink, and treat the girls with respect. And be careful."

Benny said this every time we walked out of his store, but because I knew who he was, *how* he was, it never seemed like he was preaching at me. He just cared and didn't want us to make the same mistakes he had. He even called the counselors and vice principals to ask how we were doing. They called him before they called Ángel or Smiley's mother whenever one of them got into trouble. If either of them got suspended, and they called him about it, Benny made them work at the store and would do his best not to make it fun by making them stock the cooler or clean the toilet.

FIFTEEN

As soon as we went outside, I wished we were back in Benny's store with the air-con keeping us cool. There weren't any clouds and the sun was shining down hard, just like it almost always did in the Valley. I started sweating right away.

"Oye, güey," Ángel said, "Let's go check out the tags over on the wall. I heard there was something new." We walked up Bonham a little bit to the wall of this office supply store that had the whitest walls, where kids tagged and they painted over them with many coats of white paint. Just like that, tags and white paint over them, over and over again. The storeowners would not give up and neither did the taggers. Ángel always said there was nothing prettier than a white wall. I guess he meant it was like seeing a blank sheet of paper where you're going to draw something. It's like anything can happen. You can put your mark any which way.

On the wall were the messy tags and next to them were the tagging crew names. The taggers were winning the war on the wall right now, but whoever it was that owned the store, would paint it white very soon. I never understood why they didn't put up surveillance cameras or something. I guess they were as stubborn as the taggers, that they wouldn't give up no matter what.

I said, "Hey, look at that." The rival gang in Dennett, the Ochos, had spray-painted *HCP* upside-down, using their color. To write HCP upside-down like that meant down with HCP, that all HCPs should be dead. They were called Ochos because they lived over there on eight-mile line. The tags they made were nothing like the tagging crews'. They were made without pride or style at all. The way each tagging crewer made their name, you could tell who each one was and you had to smile each time you saw their name. Taggers like Trooper and Serch wrote their names in their own ways, crossing out other taggers' names. But to them, crossing someone else's name meant just that they were doing battle for space and names, but no one would get blasted. Their biggest thing was getting their name in the most visible, but hardest-to-get-to place, on walls and overpasses where it would be easy for them to get caught.

Ángel said, "Some little esquincle junior high kids did this." Truth was, Ángel never really cared about the tags. He thought they were for little kid wannabes, and said if you were for real, the only tag to prove it was the one you put on yourself. Ángel just liked watching the show of it.

As we turned around, we saw a white Honda cruising down Bonham real slow.

I said, "Guess who it is."

Rey and Eddie were in the front seat and their music was thumping and they kept looking our way. With the windows rolled down, I could see their faces. It was like they were looking for us. I guess I had been waiting for this since we threw down on Eddie at the Red Carpet Inn.

I said, "What do you want to do, güey?"

"Just stay here with me, Güero, and whatever you do, keep looking at them."

If we had had Rigo with us, he would have thrown HCP or yelled across the street at them, but Ángel never threw signs. Everybody knew him, how he claimed HCP as his identity. He didn't have to throw anything or draw any tags on walls. He had tagged himself, with HCP on his neck. Ángel didn't even have to lift the chin or do anything. If he didn't like you, he would just look right through you or smile at you in a way that said he owned you.

I knew because before Ángel and I were friends, this was how he looked at me.

Back at the beginning of junior high, when Ángel and Smiley and all the kids came from different elementaries didn't know each other yet, Ángel and the other junior high HCPs would run around the playground during lunch and PE, being a bunch of montoneros, beating up any kids who hadn't claimed any gang for themselves, kids who were on their own like me. They would beat us up just for fun, never too bad, but just bad enough so everyone would know who controlled.

This one time they started chasing me, the private school kid, and this kid named Danny Barrera, a friend I had made in PE. You *had* to have friends, *especially* in PE. When they got close to me I got sick of it and stopped. I just started kicking and punching all psycho, my pop's voice telling me not to stay in one place, because if they got a hold of me it would be all over. I shuffled side to side like a boxer so I wouldn't fall over my feet, like Pop taught me to do. Pop would always say, *If there's going to be a fight, and you know there's going to be a fight, you got to throw first. If it's a bunch of montoneros, you got to keep moving, don't let them hold you. If they hold you, it's all over. You're done.* Those HCPs started backing off because I was kicking them gacho and some of them were down on the dirt holding onto their stomachs, and the rest scattered like cucarachas. The others were just standing there not sure what to do, watching me all surprised that somebody had actually fought back. *No one* ever fought back.

Then it was just me and Ángel standing, looking at each other. Even then in eighth grade Ángel was a lot bigger than me. He punched me in the cheek and I tried to act all tough, smiling about it, acting like it didn't hurt, even though it made my whole head shake. I didn't hit back though. I just stood there.

Hit me again, I said, pointing to the other side of my face, trying not to let them hear my voice shaking. *Maybe you can actually hit me hard with the other hand?* The truth was now that I had stopped fighting *all* of them I was all scared to fight just *one* of them, especially Ángel. Because if he threw a good one and I looked stupid, then I wouldn't have an excuse for getting discounted in front of the whole school.

He hit me in the same spot instead and it stung more. I said, *Otra vez. Is that all you got? I'll take your best shot.*

Oye éste, Ángel said looking around at everybody and hit me the last time. This time it was in the nose and my eyes started to water and my nose started to run with blood and mocos. I spit and wiped my nose but didn't cry and I never looked away from his eyes. Ángel wasn't the first one to teach me this lesson. *You look away, you're telling them that you're afraid, that you're weak,* Pop had said, talking about when you are weighing in with the other fighter or about those seconds when you're facing off as the referee goes over the rules.

I stood there. Then Ángel held out his hand to shake mine. *You're all right. You're all right, Güero.* It was the first time I'd been called *Güero. Bien psycho killer and you don't even know it. Brown and proud even if you do look like a gabachito. Güero.*

From then on he left me alone and even started talking to me in the halls, and all of the other HCP vagos would give me a lot of space when I walked near them. Soon me and Ángel and Smiley were friends, eating lunch and skipping classes together. He taught me that all that throwing down on the playground was because you had to show force. You had to scare others into respecting you or you would be the one getting chased, that if you didn't take the fight to them, that they brought it you in the way *they* wanted it to go down. *The first part to winning,* he said, *was making sure you were the one to decide how, where, and when it went down.*

Everybody called me Güero after that and they said it with respect, not like they would say it to a gringo. I was the only kid in the whole school who had ever stood up to Ángel and everyone knew it. To them, I was the one who didn't feel pain, who wasn't afraid of anyone, not even the biggest, meanest kid in the school. I was Güero at school and Cirilo at home. Names are like blood, giving us life and pride, telling us who we are. I now had two, one from each of my familias.

Eddie and Rey went down the street a ways and then pulled into a parking lot to come back around to our side of the street. I watched them roll up, ready to hit the sidewalk if they started throwing bullets at us. What I couldn't figure out was why we were just standing there. I knew Ángel never showed fear to anyone, but this just wasn't smart. If they did have cuetes, we were just sitting out in the open. All we had to do was walk away, back through the alley into the Economy and everything would be okay. That's all we had to do, but why was Ángel just making us stand there?

"What do you want to do, güey?"

"Cálmate, just wait until they get closer." Ángel knew something he wasn't telling me.

They got closer and Eddie in the passenger seat was messing around with something at his feet. It looked like he was trying to tie his shoes, but I knew that wasn't it. He had a cuete. Just as I was about to run past the store into the alley, Ángel lifted his T-shirt and I could see a black pistol grip. Where did he get a pistol from?

Ángel lifted his chin at Eddie and Rey. They could see it too because Eddie stopped messing with whatever was at his feet and they sped up and passed us, not even looking at us. They weren't going to blast us, because they knew Ángel would blast them too.

Sweat was going all down my back and my throat was dry, but I tried to sound all cold-blooded when I said, "It's on, güey. It's on." I watched the Honda go down Bonham.

It was on. The feelings I sometimes got—that I would lose these friends I had, Ángel and Smiley—they were on. The way I could never see a future—one where Ángel and Smiley and me got older and stayed friends—it was on. Losing the people who were closer than blood to me. It was on. It was on because of what we had done to Eddie at the Red Carpet Inn, and whatever happened next, was on all of us, *montoneros* all, jumping Eddie together, putting all of this in motion. It was on me, just like Perla getting jumped had been, and this was moving on its own, and I couldn't stop it, even if I wanted to. In the middle of all this was Llorona, her smile fading into darkness for some reason I didn't know yet.

I stood there looking at Ángel, his eyes like slits. Then I thought again about how Ángel and I met. If I'd tried to throw down one-on-one with Ángel like that, he would have taken me down, made me look weak. But instead I took everything he had, all his strength from each punch. This way all those montoneros knew he couldn't beat me down. *That's* why he had shaken my hand, out of the fear he couldn't beat me no matter what he did, out of the fear that everybody watching would know that for those couple of minutes I was stronger than he was. Ángel had been more scared than I was back then, but right now, with the way I was shaking inside and how I felt cold even with how hot it was, I wasn't sure who was more afraid.

SIXTEEN

THE MUSIC WAS ON, thumping, vibrating down to our bones. It was Monday night, teen night in the Attik at Klub X, the club in McAllen where upstairs they played Hip Hop and downstairs they played techno. We were all standing around, me, Smiley, Ángel, Monstruo, and Bobby, and a bunch of other homies from Dennett. Over the music Ángel was again telling the story of what had happened.

Ángel said, "You should a seen them all cagados." Here he acted like a scared girl, waving his arms all stupid.

We were all laughing and slapping hands together.

"Right," Ángel said, "Tell them, Güero. Tell them how they were all scared, driving off all fast, todos volados y cagados."

Somebody said, "HCP *love!*" This made me look around to see if any vatos from Pharr were around, but I didn't see anyone we knew. The thing was, we wouldn't know who they were even if we saw them. Everybody looked like we did, all of us dressed the same in baggy shirts and pants, standing around with those fluorescent medical bracelets that told everybody we were under twenty-one.

"Yeah, güey, that's right."

Llorona was out on the floor dancing with her girls, Brenda and Gladis. I was glad güey Rey or Eddie wasn't around, because it could get ugly in here quick. You couldn't bring a cuete or a knife in the Attik because these big vatos at the door patted you down, so that left all the fights inside the Attik being all out, fists and feet everywhere.

The floor was full, lots of bump and grind and no room at all. I said, "Güey Rey," real quiet, but then laughed out loud.

"What're you laughing at?" Smiley said.

"Güey Rey. Get it. I'm a poet and I didn't know it."

"You're *all* messed up, güey. ¿Cómo andas?"

"Ando bien," I said, meaning I was fine.

"Olvídate, ya. Forget about him and forget about Llorona. She and Brenda said they weren't even talking to them anymore, that they were never really tight with them to begin with, and she's more like third cousins with Eddie anyways." He said this last part because he could see the way I was looking at her, that even as I was talking to him, my eyes were on her the whole time. I knew it was a lie. Llorona and Brenda had said all of that so that people wouldn't start saying they weren't loyal, that she and Brenda were the kind who went with other vatos from other neighborhoods.

But I couldn't forget her, how she had been with Rey, what she'd done to me long ago, how it had all played out here in the Attik. How *everybody* had seen her make me look stupid. I'd run out like some punk and *everybody* had seen. Why was it that anytime the lights were low or off, this came back to me even stronger. Why did the darkness bring back what was ugly?

The night long ago that ended everything with me and Llorona, I got there late because Ángel had wanted to cruise around with his cousin first and drink a couple quarts before we even got to Klub X. We were supposed to meet the girls there because they'd gone early so they could dance all they wanted.

I walked in all smiles, all stupid, not knowing what I was about to see.

I saw Llorona dancing and at first, I thought she was out there with her girls, but I got closer and saw what was up. This maniác from I still don't know where was holding her *real* close, his hands around her where only mine belonged. Her hand was in his hair, playing with it. I got this sick feeling and I moved up to them fast, my fists closing and opening. I was ready to throw down hard to kill him.

I got closer and then Llorona saw me. She looked real deep into my eyes, but her eyes were like glass. This wasn't the worst part, though. It was the way she smiled at me, like she was happy she'd finally gotten back at everyone who had ever hurt her: her mother, her father, and the man, her mother's boyfriend, who'd made her try to kill herself. It was the smile of La Llorona when she kills, the black evil spirit Llorona had inside of her. I'd always told her that no, she was really good inside, that she'd just been hurt too many times, and she didn't have something evil inside of her, but that night I finally believed her. I couldn't look into those eyes and believe anything else.

And you know, she could have walked to me, said she was sorry, she didn't mean it, and I would have thrown down on this fool, and it would have been all over. But the way she looked at me hurt me more than fists or knives or bullets. All I could do was walk away, walk out like a cobarde, a nothing. I don't know how I got out of Klub X that night because all the strength was gone from my body as I kept thinking of them together, his skin on hers.

All of this was playing in my head as I watched Llorona out there now moving to that music wearing a white T-shirt that made her glow. The dance floor was bathed in this blue light, and all of the dancers around her looked like they were dancing underwater. Llorona was in the center, glowing, moving her hands above her, waving the others in to join her in the water, each of the dancers drowning and writhing and not caring she was pulling them under with her. Her body was like liquid in the way that none of her moves were out of rhythm, and she seemed to be moving in slow motion. Her eyes were closed like always, and she was thinking about something, maybe seeing a vision from the past or something that was about to happen. I watched to see if she would open her eyes and a couple of times when she did, I thought I saw her looking at me.

Then a slow song came on and everybody cleared the dance floor. All except Llorona and her girls and some couples. Whenever Llorona and her friends went to teen night, they were on the dance floor almost the whole time except for when they went to the bathroom together. Llorona once told me, *Why pay cover if all you're going to do is just stand around? I could do that at home for free.*

Smiley asked me, "Hey, where you going?" but I didn't say anything to him as I left Ángel and all of them, stepping into the water with her. It seemed like someone was always asking where I was going, trying to stop me from drowning myself under Llorona's embrace.

Llorona was out there and she looked *at* me then, not through me like a ghost she couldn't see, but like I was a dead person who had come back to life and *I* had been the ghost the whole time, not her. On her face was the guilt I'd wanted back then, the look that said, *I wish I could take it all back. Please forgive me, my Güero.*

With her eyes on mine, all the time we'd been dead to each other *hadn't* happened and none of this, the club or the smoke or all the locos, were even around. Llorona didn't know what was on my mind, how when I first started walking out there, I'd wanted to embarrass her bad, make *her* look like an idiota like I had. But each step I took was like someone else was taking it, taking me deeper underwater to be with my Llorona.

Now it was just me and her and the music. Brenda and Gladis walked away because they knew. I reached for Llorona's waist. It was so small I could hold her with both hands and my fingers could almost touch. I had wanted to throw my hand in her face, tell everyone I wasn't having any of her. I wanted everyone to know that she was too evil for me, but Llorona always had her way. In the end, Llorona always pushed you down in the water with her no matter how hard you fought. And this was the only way you wanted it to be.

Let me tell you a secret, she said without speaking out loud, waving me over to her with her finger.

I leaned my ear toward her mouth and she kissed it, a little kiss like only she knew how to give. In her breath I thought I could hear *I love you*, but I wasn't sure. Llorona used to say, *A kiss is a secret between two souls together.* Now I understood. We kissed now and we shared our separate sadnesses, changed one for the other. This was the only way life was worth it. This was how we fought our feeling that life wasn't supposed to be like it was: Llorona with her father gone with another woman up North, her childhood taken away by some animal, and her mother a bruja who made magic that only hurt people, and my parents, who I saw drinking, drunk, or crudos more times than I saw them sober, if I even saw them.

The others, they didn't understand what was happening. They whistled loud at us, louder than the music, like I was just trying to get some. But no one knew my Llorona like I did. They'd never seen the notes or the poems she wrote. She drew these thorny roses and hearts with arrows in them on the margins of the paper of her composition book and the notes she wrote me. I could never explain how she was when we were alone. No one deserved to know how we used to lay on her couch when her mother wasn't there or locked in her room. They couldn't know how my Llorona would scratch my head with those long, decorated nails of hers and tell me about secrets from her life, how it would be when we got older.

We'll buy a house and you'll take over your dad's business, and we'll wake up together and all of this, she said, looking around at her smelly, dirty house, *will only be a bad dream I can't even remember. You'll be my old man and I'll take care of you till I'm a viejita and my skin's all saggy and I'm all chimuela smiling at you with windows where my teeth used to be.* As she said all this I couldn't picture this future. I could never see my girl turning old and I think she didn't believe herself either.

But now while I'm young and beautiful, mi Cirilo, you can have mil besos. She moved her eyelashes all dramatic like one of those actresses from the telenovelas on Univisión and gave me *mil besos*, kissing me all over my face and neck. Each kiss made my body feel warm, and it made me forget everyone in the whole world was still alive.

When my friends asked me why I put up with her, I never said any of this. They just wouldn't understand.

I could hear the song now that it was almost over, and I took her off of the floor before it did. This way, I thought, it was like the song didn't really end.

Later Llorona and I sat there, watching everyone like we used to, as if only a day had passed since the last time we had done this. Llorona and I could just sit and watch people and laugh at the little things they did for hours. A lot of times when we were at parties or the mall, this was all we did. The funny thing was, we always noticed and laughed at the same things, like right now how we were watching this one fool move from girl to girl, asking to dance and getting an ugly look every time.

Ángel was out on the dance floor between Brenda and Gladis. He had his big smile on, and Smiley was over by the bar trying to buy a Coke for some big white girl named Katie from McAllen. Any time Smiley saw her he had to put the move on. Again, she wasn't having any. He was all jealous because Ángel was dancing with Brenda and he wasn't and he was trying to substitute for the real thing.

Llorona was sitting on my lap and I was holding her, my arms around her waist. We were quiet in front of the others like we used to be, and everybody left us alone, doing their own thing. I wondered the time, knowing our time together was passing. I got this feeling like this wasn't going to last. I tried not to think about it, tried to blame my mother's superstition of never saying goodbye. I didn't want to ruin what was happening now so I could enjoy each moment I was given with Llorona before it all went away again.

Smiley came up to us. "Now ésa, she's what I call a BBBW. You got the BBW, the Big Beautiful Woman like Brenda. But that baby doll, she's a Bien Buena Big Beautiful Woman. That baby doll, she's going to be my girl. I got a feeling."

I said, "That's not enough Bs. You mean 4BW. Because you got B for Bien, B for Buena…."

"Whatever, güey, you know what I was saying."

Llorona laughed for real, not all gacha like she had at the park. "Por favor, Smiley. You know Brenda loves you. You're the only man for her."

"Don't mess with me like that."

"Why would I lie? She thinks you're chulito."

"Don't play me. You know how I am with Brenda."

"Yeah, *I* know, but how's *she* going to know if you don't say anything? How's she going to know if you're always joking around about it. You need to tell her for real."

Then Smiley got this look like he had never thought of this in his whole life.

"¿Sabes qué? You're right." He looked away like he was thinking about what to say.

To Llorona I said, "Oye you're not lying, right? Don't mess with him like that."

She looked at me, her eyes saying, *Por favor, why would I lie?*

SEVENTEEN

AFTER OUR TIME AT the Attik, we were at the Whataburger in Dennett and Ángel ordered, "A double meat, double cheese combo, super size, a Whataburger Junior, a regular Whataburger, no lettuce, no pickles. Are you all selling breakfast taquitos yet? Yeah? Well then give me a potato, egg, and cheese. You all want anything else? You sure? Yeah, that'll be all."

Ángel got out this big roll to pay and I figured he'd been doing some more stereo work for his cousin Fernando. Besides Fernando, Ángel could install stereos faster and cleaner than anybody I knew.

Brenda was up there at the counter standing with Smiley, her head on his shoulder, all over him like they were going around. At the club, he had asked Brenda outside so she could talk to him. They had been gone for a long time and when they came back in, they were holding hands. I was happy for him. Smiley had been after her for a long time. I hadn't had a chance to ask him what he said.

It was just us six at Whataburger now: me, Ángel, Smiley, Gladis, Brenda, and Llorona. At this hour, on a Monday night in Dennett, everyone else was asleep.

We were all sitting in a booth except for Smiley and Brenda who were still up at the counter waiting for the order. Ángel pointed his chin at the counter and said, "Mira, look at my baby brother and Brenda. Don't they look cute? My carnalito finally hooked up with her. Listen, watch."

Gladis said, "No Ángel, don't say anything."

Ángel sucked his teeth at her and said it anyway. "Oye, you two up there. Oye, Number Ten!"

I said, "Number Ten? What're you talking about?" Just then, Llorona went to the restroom and the way she did it, fast without saying anything, I thought maybe she was mad at Ángel for making fun of them. All the way from Klub X, as she had sat in my lap in the backseat of Brenda's car, she had been saying that everything was complete now. I wish I had paid more attention to what she said, because I was about to find out what she meant.

"Mira, he's the number one and she's the zero." They all looked at them and busted out laughing. Ángel was gacho saying that, pointing that out, Smiley being all skinny like a number 1 and Brenda all gordita like a 0.

"Oye Number Ten, tell them to hurry up with our food. Or we're all going to have to call you the couple called Number Eleven if Brenda doesn't get her food soon."

Brenda turned around and gave him the look.

"Hey Brenda, what sign you throwing now? Is that the Number 10 Crew? Smiley *love*."

I saw the look on Smiley's face, how aguitado his brother was making him, and I said, "Cálmate, déjalo. He finally hooked up."

"Pues, 'ta bueno," he said. Ángel could be *real* gacho once he got started making fun of his brother. He'd always been that way. No one else could make fun of him, but he could go on all day with it. For some reason though, Ángel always listened to me when I told him to leave Smiley alone.

They were eating, not saying a thing, yellow burger paper everywhere, the fancy ketchup cups turned upside down, salt and pepper sticking to their elbows and Llorona was still in the restroom. The food we had ordered sat in the bag. I only took out some fries and ate them, but I didn't get out my hamburger because I was waiting for Llorona. If you got your food before your girl did, you were supposed to wait for her. This was another of the things Pop had taught me because he never ate until Mama also had a plate in front of her.

Smiley was the only one who could never shut up, even when he was eating. Ángel could never stop saying mean things, and Smiley could never be quiet. It was like they were both afraid of silence. Their father had to have been the one they got it from, because their mother never said too much at all.

Smiley said, "If I decide to go on a three-state killing and bank robbing spree, and I'm on death row, Whataburger's going to be the last thing I eat. I'll tell the warden, 'Lobster ni que lobster. Forget about that noise. Give me a double meat Whataburger with cheese, no pickles, no onions, with chingos of jalapeños.' Hey, Carnál. Did you tell them no onions? I just bit into a big fat piece of raw onion. What's up with that?"

"Just take it out, Carnál. Quit your complaining already. Just let us eat. *Nunca te callas*. And three-state killing spree? Texas is pretty big bro. Do you know how much driving that would be for it to be a *three-state* killing spree? It takes at least ten hours to get out of Texas. You'd fall asleep before you got to Houston, and besides, you couldn't hurt a fly."

Smiley said, "How would *you* know anyway? You've never even been out of Texas. The farthest you've been is San Antonio."

Ángel just sucked his teeth because he had nothing to say about that.

Llorona was still in the bathroom and I had that feeling you get when the person you're with is away from you. You want so bad for them to hurry up, to come back to your side, bring their warmth back to you where it belongs.

Just as I was going to ask Brenda or Gladis to go check on her, Llorona came back and I made room in the booth for her, but she didn't sit down.

Her face was serious and if I didn't know better, I would've thought she had been crying. She said "Güero? Tengo que decirte algo."

What did she have to tell me? *It's about Rey*, I thought. Whatever it was, I didn't want to hear it. Everyone in the booth went quiet.

"Can you come outside to talk to me?"

My first thought was to tell her no, to tell her we were fine sitting here because this was always Smiley and Ángel's complaint about her, that she took me away from everyone, that she had to have all of my time and attention.

"¿Sabes qué," I said. "Let's just not talk about anything. All right? Let's just sit here and be like old times. Don't you think? What do you think?" This was a good in-between thing to say, not telling her no, but not telling her yes either.

She wouldn't let it go, even though right then there was nothing I wanted more. I looked at Brenda and Gladis to give me backup on this, but they just looked away. They weren't going to do that for anything. Llorona gave me the ojitos, like only she could, the little eyes that were part begging, part telling me she would tear me apart if I didn't do what she asked.

We stood outside now, and I told her, "What is it?" It was still hot outside even though it was after midnight.

Llorona said, "I have to tell you something and it's not all about Rey. Ese güey, no vale. You know he's not worth it, don't you? I was just being a pichona, letting him buy me clothes and stuff. No, ésto, the thing I got to say is kind of about Rey, but more about something else." What could be worse than that? I thought.

"Pues, 'ta bueno. Tell me." It was good to hear Rey didn't matter to her. I looked into her eyes to listen, but she looked away and didn't say anything else. "Tell me," I said again.

"This thing I have to say. You have to be serious. You have to listen."

"Okay, okay. I'm listening."

"Güero, I've been thinking a lot about you, and a lot's happened between us. It's all crazy, you know. You know?"

I nodded that I knew, that all of this time apart should have never happened.

Llorona said, "What I want to say is I'm sorry for what I did all that time ago. I'm sorry for how it seemed like I didn't even care.

Because I regretted it afterward. I knew I had made the biggest mistake of my life."

Why did she have to bring it up? I rolled my eyes and looked away from her.

She went on. "I told you before, I was all messed up. Y ese güey, he was just a punk. I don't even remember his name. The only reason I did it was because I destroy everyone and everything and I knew this was the only way to push you out, to save you from me. I thought that to stay with you was a curse worse than hurting you. You are the only good I have ever known." This was supposed to make me feel better?

She seemed to know what I was thinking because she said, "This might not make you feel better or be the apology that you wanted but these are things you have to know."

Llorona grabbed my face and turned me toward her.

"But there's something else, something *very* important."

"What else?" I said through my teeth. Why did there have to be more? There was always more with her.

"You know those times when you saw me with Rey? I already told you I was just being a pichona, but I didn't tell you why. You know it's not like me to be like that. The reason I was doing that was for money, not for love. I got some serious feria out of him because I need it."

With all the blood going to my face, she saw all the thoughts playing like a movie. Llorona said, "No, no, no, don't worry, it's not like that. I got the money for a different reason, something you won't understand, but I just want you to know I never let him touch me like you did. ¿Entiendes?"

The words *like you did* played out in my head and I wished she had ended her sentence with, *I never let him touch me.* I got it together and asked her, "Why did you need money?"

"It's hard to explain, but if I tell you, you got to promise not to tell, or it'll mess everything up."

Just then they all walked out, Smiley and Brenda looking so funny together because she was taller than he was. He had his arm around her, his arm up high. Smiley looked happy to be letting the whole world know she was his queen, and up until that moment, I didn't know he could smile any bigger than he usually did.

I knew it was time for us to go, but I needed to know what she was talking about. Gladis and Brenda had to get home before their fathers woke up for work. Besides, Brenda had borrowed her mother's car, telling her she was going to the movies. The rest of us, we knew it didn't matter, but we didn't want them getting into trouble, even though they probably would.

Brenda gave us more time by telling Smiley, "Hey Chulito, come over to my car. I want to show you something. Bring their food too."

We leaned against the car as they all four sat inside with the stereo pumping.

Her chin was in my fingers.

"Díme, tell me what you were going to say."

"I'll tell you later. I promise. I promise I'll tell you everything." Llorona *never* made promises.

"Tomorrow when I see you, how's it going to be?"

"How you want it to be. Siempre he estado aquí, esperandote, aguantando mi vida sin tu amor." Somehow I knew she was lying, even though she could look God in the face and lie without looking away from his eyes. I didn't know what she was lying about, whether tomorrow would be how I wanted it or if she had always been waiting around for me, barely making it without my love.

Whatever I wanted. This was what I wanted to believe. So this is what I told her.

I said, "What I want my Llorona is for this, for *all* of this to not end. I want us to be together like this always. You in my arms. What we have right now, I want it to last. So what I'm saying is tomorrow I want it to be like it is now, better than old times, better than anything we imagined."

Llorona looked so sad, like she knew something I didn't.

"¿Qué pasó? What is it? Just tell me what's wrong."

"Nada." *Nothing* was Llorona's favorite word when *something* was wrong.

So I played it off like I usually did. "Pues 'ta bueno. Tomorrow it's going to be all good y este amor, this love we got, it's not going to be just something from our imaginations. Do you believe that?"

Llorona looked straight into my eyes and said, "Sí es cierto." I knew this was a lie and Llorona didn't believe it to be true. She put her hand to my forehead and it was warm, warmer than I remembered. She put her head to my chest and said something I couldn't hear.

"What?" I said.

"Nada, Cirilo. It's all good. Everything's going to be good for you now." Again, the word *nothing*. She had wet eyes like glass and she bit her lip to hide the way it was shaking. Something was up because she *never* cried. The only tears any of us saw were the ones painted in blue on the insides of her eyes.

"¿Qué pasó? Tell me what's wrong." This was her way. The more I asked, the less she wanted to tell me what she was thinking. "No llores mi Llorona, I'll see you tomorrow, and we'll go say hi to Benny at the Economy. I'll have Benito hook you up with a burrito, and then we can go walking around. Sound good?" She actually smiled at the thought of both of us seeing Benny together.

"Yeah, it does." She got on her tiptoes to kiss me and her lips were hot and soft like a crying girl's, except there weren't any tears in her eyes. Just the wet eyes like she was about to.

She said, "Un beso como un secreto." Her kiss was like a secret between us, how we shared something we never told anyone about because they would never understand.

Ángel and Smiley got out of the car and Llorona got in the back seat. I leaned into the window. She didn't say anything and just looked up at me with her sad eyes.

When we were together and we would say good-bye, I always got this feeling I wouldn't see her again. Except with her it was stronger than I ever felt it for anyone else. That feeling like the good thing you got is going to be taken away from you. I didn't know what Llorona was hiding, but did she know the secret *I* had passed onto *her*, this feeling that something real bad was about to happen to all of us?

I wanted to lean in, hold her a little longer. Then as they drove away, I wanted her to look out the back window, to wave good-bye or something. The last I saw of her was her black hair pulled up, the soft back of her neck, her face away from me looking forward to somewhere, to some time in the future where I wasn't.

EIGHTEEN

Since it was a Monday night, not too many people were out on the streets. Smiley was in the middle between me and Ángel. He was so happy he didn't care where he sat, and *I* had window this time.

I said, "So you all going around or what?"

"Pues a ver que pasa, we'll see what happens. Esa Brenda she's bien buena, and I can't explain these feelings."

Ángel said, "Carnál, careful with her. She tears men apart."

"Shut it, that's my baby doll you're talking about. I'm going to have to kick your nalgas, but I mean ugly. You don't want that. Right, Güero?"

"It's true. He's going to take you to school if you don't shut your mouth. Once Smiley's motivated, you better watch out. All this boy needs is ganas."

Ángel laughed. "Yeah, he's got chingos of ganas now."

Then Ángel said, "And what's up with you and Llorona? I thought you were going to forget about her." The way he said it made me think of all the times he told me to break up with her and find someone else. Pretty much from the beginning, Ángel didn't like Llorona. He said that she had me whipped, that all she had to do was say *how high*, and I would jump, that I would carry her purse in the mall. He went on and on about it. This was another list of Ángel's that kept going. When he got through with this list, he said that she had changed me. Because of this, Ángel barely talked to her.

I said, "Me and Llorona tonight? Didn't mean nothing. I was just playing with her, seeing what I could get."

Smiley rolled his eyes. "Whatever, güey, I saw how you were, all in love with the happy eyes and the stupid smile. You know you never got over her. You may have talked like you were all bad, but you were always thinking about her."

"For real, güey, I was just playing her."

I looked over at Ángel to see if he was going to play this game with us, but he wasn't having any of it. He just looked ahead at the road and did not say anything.

We drove, and then we were at a stop light on Bonham in Dennett. A car was rolling up behind us with its high beams on.

Ángel said, "Oye, what's their problem? They trying to blind me or what?"

I looked in the side mirror and the car changed lanes and the beams were those blue ones, the halogen ones that give you a headache when you look straight into them. I got the idea to get back at Smiley and Ángel for making the stupid joke at the mall where I looked like Ángel's novio. As soon as this car rolled up, I leaned forward and looked up at Smiley and Ángel's faces.

"Who looks stupid now?" I said.

Smiley said, "Hey güey, get up. That's a lowrider. We might know those vatos and forget it if they see me and Ángel sitting like this together. Get up." He started laughing too and then punching me in the ribs, which made me laugh harder.

Then, all of a sudden, Smiley's face changed. The street lights made his face look yellow. There were shadows and seriousness in his face like I had never seen and it should have made me stay down. But I picked my head up and looked out the window to look at what had scared Smiley. It happened so fast I don't remember what car, what face. All I remember seeing was an arm coming out of a white car, a cuete pointing our way, and hearing nothing, as if the sound was turned off. I didn't have time to duck back down. Ángel and

Smiley ducked down, and there I was, stupid me, with my head out in the open, waiting to get blasted.

And then I heard the pop, pop, pop, so much louder than I thought a gun was, a cuete going off so close to my ear. Then tires peeling out, a car driving away. It looked like a Honda, but I couldn't be sure.

I said, "Hey, you all right, you all right, you all right? I'm good, I think." I patted myself down looking for any blood because I heard that people could get shot and not know it right away.

"Yeah, güey, we're all right. Good thing we ducked in time. Could a gotten blasted." It was Ángel talking.

"Hey, Smiley. You all right?"

Ángel said, "Carnalito, get up, they're gone. Quit being all scared. Get up, they're gone." Ángel pushed Smiley and he still didn't move.

I said, "A con una Smiley, quit messing around, güey. Ya, get off me." He was leaning over me and I shook him. It was then that I saw the blood on the back of his white T-shirt, which didn't look red, but brown in the street lights.

"Ya, güey. Get up! Quit playing around, get up." Ángel was shaking him hard now, telling him to stop it, quit playing, and his voiced started to shake, and then it was like I was watching the whole thing from somewhere else. I was talking, saying the same things Ángel was, but it was like I was hearing someone else say them, like I was floating up above all of this. Right then I prayed to God I could *be* somebody else.

God didn't listen because it was me, Güero, who then did what it seemed like I was watching someone else do. It was me Güero, who reached in the glove box and pulled out Ángel's .25, ran out of the truck over to the pay phone at the Burger King, calling for an ambulance. Me, Güero, on the phone, trying real hard to remember where I was at because everything looked so different to me, like I wasn't even in Dennett. Me, Güero, who had made his best friend Smiley get shot. Me who had the gun now, running in the opposite direction, away from Smiley and Ángel, not even knowing if Smiley was alive or dead.

NINETEEN

I WALKED IN THE shadows, hiding behind trees and cars whenever I saw headlights or heard a car come close.

When the chotas got to Ángel, they'd be asking him all kinds of questions and everything would come back to me, the one who had called, the one who was gone.

Maybe Ángel would see that I'd taken his .25, maybe not. If he did see, he wouldn't say anything to the chotas about it. He would just smile through his tears and say nothing but Smiley's name. It would be like a prayer to him, the only thing keeping him from showing the chota the wet eyes. Was Smiley alive?

I had to walk through the neighborhoods because Bonham was a big road with lots of lights, and I'd either get busted or shot, depending on who saw me.

Even though I could feel the sweat on my back, down my neck, I was glad it was a hot night with no wind. This way I could hear everything, TVs on, dogs barking miles away, cars passing on Bonham. Was Smiley dead?

Then I was in the silence of Herrera Road, the silence of my house, the refrigerator hum, the air-con kicking on, my breath, the sound of Pop's work keys so loud like chains, the sound of night just before it becomes morning.

I didn't take his truck, but the white van he had out in the back, the same one I had taken to Bell's. I tried pushing it out so I could start it away from the house, but forget it, the van was too heavy and it made my legs shake and feel weak.

I was gone even though I didn't know where I was going, even though I knew I should have been wherever Smiley and Ángel were. I didn't know where Rey or Eddie lived, only that they were from somewhere in Pharr. One time I'd driven through the worst part of their neighborhood with Pop, on one of those days when he was trying out a new restaurant he'd heard about, so I figured that was as good of a place to start as any. I jacked the .25, put a bullet into the chamber, just like Pop had shown me once when he took me shooting out at a ranch in Edinburg. *When you shoot a pistol, you got to let it surprise you. Don't expect it to go off. If you do that, it messes up your shot.* Why hadn't any of the bullets hit me? Pop, pop, pop, at least one hitting Smiley who should have been protected by the door, the other two going who knows where. My head was out in the open, but nothing had hit me, and suddenly I understood. Rey or Eddie had aimed for the door, maybe not meaning to kill us, but one of the bullets went through, and since Smiley had ducked, it hit him.

I just had to find that white Honda.

I drove up and down the streets of Pharr for what seemed like hours, looking for them. Only a few cars were out now. Then I turned off and started driving through the neighborhood streets. Lights were off in all of the houses up and down the neighborhood. I looked at parked cars in the streets and driveways for the white Honda.

And then, just as I was thinking I should forget about it, just go home or to the hospital, I saw a white car backed into a driveway that looked like a Honda. I rolled up slow and saw shadows in the porch of the house, little cherries from cigarettes, shiny cans of beer catching the light, but no faces. I grabbed the .25, made sure about the safety, and started to point it out the window, rolling real slow as I got into range, but something didn't seem right.

The shadows moved into the orange street light and then I saw their faces, Eddie and Rey and lots of other vatos I didn't recognize.

They threw their signs, held their hands out wide in challenge and I saw some of them carrying cuetes. *¿Y qué?* their hands said, waiting for me to answer. *So what are you going to do? What are you going to throw?* They had been waiting for us to do something like this.

And what? their hands said, still waiting for my answer. *What are you going to do?* All of them standing there with their arms out were afraid too. It was easier for them to stand together like montoneros challenging me. Alone, each one of them wouldn't have gotten off the porch. How many times had I seen some cobarde throwing his sign when he was standing alone, when no one was there to give him esquina? Never.

So I answered them with this: my hand dropping the gun on the dash, my foot on the pedal, taking me away. Pop's voice was in my head, saying, *A montonero is a coward. A real man can stand alone and doesn't need a montón of his friends to back him up.* Even though it was me driving away, not meeting their challenge, it was they who were the cowards.

TWENTY

As it turned out, Smiley didn't die, but as I was about to find out, people don't have to die for you to lose them forever.

For days after the shooting, I had gone to Ángel and Smiley's apartment in the Dennett Housing Authority, and no one was home. They hadn't answered their phone all the times I'd called, so I had decided to drive over there a couple of times in the van. Some people said Smiley had come home from the hospital, but none of us had seen him or even knew how he was doing.

We'd ask Ángel how he was doing and all he would say was, *He's okay*. We'd ask him to tell us more, tell us what room he was in, but that was all he would say. Ángel would get that look in his eyes when you knew to leave him alone. I'd told him I would go over to his house or the hospital to help any way I could, but any time I said this, he'd said, *No, it's better not to. I said he's okay.* I knew I had to leave it there.

Brenda couldn't wait to have Smiley come home, so she made a Welcome Home party, hoping it would bring him back to us faster. She didn't believe the rumors she was hearing. Some said Smiley was a vegetable, and you could see nothing in his eyes to tell you he was still with us. Others said he had lost all of the feeling in his body, that a piece of the bullet had torn into his spine and that all he could move were the muscles in his face. None of us knew the truth, and Ángel wasn't saying. All he said was that Smiley was fine, but you knew it wasn't true. If he had been fine, Ángel would have made fun of him somehow. He talked in this low voice and wouldn't look at any of us in the face. We had never seen this before.

Brenda said if she threw a nice-enough party, Smiley would come home. All it would take was for him to know how much everyone loved him and missed him. The thing was, I hated to admit it, but Llorona was on my mind as much as Smiley. No one had seen her after the night Smiley got shot. She wasn't answering the phone, and nobody even thought to go to her house. Llorona's mother wouldn't allow anyone over, and if she did, you could never come inside. I was the only one who had ever really been allowed inside the house. Some said Llorona wouldn't come out because she felt guilty about what had happened. Others said they thought she was afraid of getting jumped or blasted because she had been a traitor, going out with a rival from Pharr like that. The ones that felt this way said she should be called La Malinche the betrayer, not Llorona. La Malinche was the Aztec woman who sold out her people to the Spanish conquerors. They all figured she would come out when she was ready. Ángel was quiet about it, not saying what he thought about her.

The party was at Brenda's house, over on the north side by a golf course. It was nice like mine. Her parents were away on business to Monterey like they always were. In her kitchen, Brenda had hung streamers and balloons that said "Welcome Home Smiley." Ángel had showed up, and the talk was that maybe Smiley would come too. Was I the only one that knew we were lying to ourselves?

Brenda had told everyone to bring something that Smiley would like or that reminded them of him. Monstruo and Bobby brought a gold chain each and pictures Smiley had drawn of them. All Smiley's other drawings were up on the walls. Ángel had put out all the model cars we had made. Brenda gave him a piece of folded paper with a kiss on it. What was written on it was only for her and Smiley. Un beso como un secreto, a kiss like a secret.

Soon after we had looked at all the pictures and all his things, and talked about when he was coming over, we did what old people do, the men outside, the women inside, having our own separate conversations. Ángel didn't say anything the whole time. He just smiled and looked at the floor.

When we were outside, finally Ángel spoke. He said, "I remember this one time me and my carnál were *all* chuecos, walking down this alley, and this cat jumps out in front of us. Then Smiley jumps about five feet in the air. He gets down real low in this karateco stance, like he's going to start fighting with the kitty cat." I was surprised Ángel had said anything at all, but what surprised me even more was that he was talking about Smiley from the past, as if he wasn't alive.

Monstruo said, "I want to say something about Güero. Este vato, he took Ángel's cuete, and he went out looking for those fools, but he didn't find them. That's why in my opinion, he's initiated. Puro HCP por vida, you know." Monstruo really had a way of changing the subject.

Everyone except Rigo nodded with respect and threw HCP, patted me on the back, agreeing with Monstruo that I was HCP for life. Rigo was staring me down and he sucked his teeth quietly and turned away. Rigo's face was banged up and bruised, with a big knot on the side of his forehead. He had become a full HCP after all, getting jumped in for a full minute by all the locos, an initiation party I hadn't been invited to. To be a Hispanic Causing Panic, you had to be initiated, which meant you could run in a store and steal cases of beer or get the one minute beat-down, which is what they had chosen for Rigo.

Monstruo being Monstruo didn't see any of this being played out and he went on. "Este vato, he was always there for Smiley. I want him to be right there with us, pulling the trigger, giving us back-up when we do what we got to for the familia."

Somebody said, "Yeah!" Rigo sucked his teeth again in disapproval, but he wasn't about to say anything. He'd learned that at least.

Ángel pulled out a pistol from his waistband, a cuete I'd never seen him with.

"My primo knows where we can get some serious cuetes like this, not just that little .25 I had. Hey güey, you still got it?"

"Yeah, I got it at home." Actually, I had taken it apart and scattered the pieces into a canal and the bullets into a field so some kid wouldn't find it and get hurt. What I didn't say but wanted to was that gun had been the one to shoot Smiley even though it had never been fired. I couldn't even look at him right now. I didn't say it, but I started to blame Ángel for it as much as I blamed myself. Smiley had been shot because we jumped Eddie, yes, but also because Ángel had showed it to them when they drove by on Bonham. He had brought out that cuete and it had changed everything. If it had just been the beat-down we gave Eddie, maybe they would have just jumped us, or maybe they would have just shot in our direction to send a message. Ángel showing it had made sure that they would throw the bullets our way, hoping to hurt or kill us.

"Good. Keep it for a while." The sadness in his voice made me think he blamed himself too, and that he never wanted to see that .25 again.

Then something got into him, and he was going off, talking about cuetes, how his cousin Fernando could get this Tec-9 and this SKS with the butt sawed off, but all he needed was a little money. So then all of them started putting twenties and tens and fives in this cup they were passing around. The cup came to me and I knew they were looking at what each of us put in like people do in church.

I passed it on without putting anything in.

Monstruo looked at me, his face saying, *What's up with that?*

"I got nothing to give," I said.

I heard somebody blow air through their teeth. They were thinking, *'Che güey, you got chingos of money and you just don't want to give because you ain't down.*

So Ángel said, "Oyes, you stupid burros, who do you think paid for the party?"

They all went, "Oh!" like they felt stupid for what they'd been thinking. But it was a lie. I had only bought a couple of bags of chips. Ángel had paid for all the rest. Why was he lying for me?

Bobby, who was moving from side to side to the music, lifted his quart and said, "HCP *love.*"

Like we'd seen in all the movies, we all lifted our cans high and poured some out. I put my head down, watched the white foam sink into the dry ground. Nothing could grow from this. We could pour can after can our whole lives and that dry ground, it would always be dry.

I said, "Todo esto, no vale." They didn't hear me because they were all lost in their own movies of their lives. *All of this, it's not worth it.*

Brenda came out from the sliding glass door and said she wanted to take a picture with all of us, saying she wanted a memory from this night, something she could save for Smiley, to show him how much he was loved. So we all stood around, wiping the shininess off our foreheads, taking out the lagañas from the corner of our eyes.

Brenda said, "Who's going to take the picture?"

I told her I would.

They all squeezed in together. Ángel and Bobby were in front, squatting low next to each other, making the H and C. "Oyes, we need somebody to be the last letter." Ángel said. "Can't be *just HC* love."

Bobby said, "Brenda, take the picture so Güero can be the last letter."

"N'ombre, this picture is for my baby and I'm going to be in it."

"No, 'ta bien," Ángel said, "Güero'll take the picture."

Monstruo said, "N'ombre, get over here Güero, be the last one."

"No, I want Güero to *take* the picture." His voice was louder than any of us expected.

Ángel saying this and me nodding, it shut everybody up. It was like we had confessed something to them and they understood.

Monstruo said, "A con una. . . . Entonces, *tú* Rigo. *You* be the one."

Rigoberto stepped up, his dream to represent HCP come true at last. He squatted down, stared his best loco stare and made the last letter of HCP.

None of them were smiling, giving that gacho-cold stare of theirs.

"Is everybody ready?"

"Just take it, ya," Ángel said.

I looked at them all, and they couldn't see what I could, how I was right, that none of this would be worth it. They couldn't see tomorrow, when Monstruo and Bobby and Ángel would drive to Pharr and shoot into El Rey's windows with the Tec-9 and the SKS and Ángel's pistol and hit nothing but the wall and break some glass. Ángel and Monstruo and Bobby couldn't see that the thing they were about to do would be the first step that would take them all the way to the state pinta where HCP and all the rivals in the Valley didn't even matter anymore, where a lot of Valley criminals and killers became one familia, El Valluco, brothers with the same ones they'd wanted to kill, prison lifers with no hope and no future.

The flash went off and each of them rubbed their eyes like they were waking up.

"How'd we look?" Rigo said.

"Good." I said. I didn't believe my own voice.

Ángel shook hands with me and said, "Gracias por todo, carnál. You did a lot for me and my little brother. You were always my esquina. I always knew you had my back." With the way Ángel was talking about us, as if he was seeing me again after many years, I could tell that he thought his future, even though he knew how bad it was, could not be changed, that all those things the Miss had said about fate were right after all. Ángel was speaking from a place far away from this moment, where he stood without me and was looking back at who we were, knowing that this was our last time together and there would be no more memories for us to make.

I tried to pull away, but Ángel held my hand harder in the carnál handshake. He gave me one of those brother abrazos, patted my back real hard, pulled me close and whispered, "My brother is gone, carnál, he can't talk or smile or breathe on his own. Can you believe that? How can you still be alive, but be gone? My carnalito, he's gone and he's not coming back. And you're right, *none* of this is worth it, and it's not for you, *Cirilo*. It's not for you. But this is all I got, and it's all I was ever going to have." I started to speak, to tell him different, but Ángel let me go, and in this, his almost pushing me away, he told me he never wanted to see me come around again.

TWENTY-ONE

WHEN I WALKED AWAY from Brenda's house, no one but Ángel noticed. They were all still doing their thing, lost in their own dramas. I just wanted to stand in the quiet for a second, get away from the thoom-thoom of the music going through my body. The chicharras were still buzzing and the cool night wind was out, blowing dirt and mowed grass around.

I had planned to go back inside, but I found that I kept walking, past all the different neighborhoods, and I didn't really know where I was going. I just wanted to get away from there.

Then I was looking for Llorona. I went to Bonham Hill Cemetery first, the place she used to go when she wanted to be alone, even though it was the furthest away from Brenda's. She also went there whenever she ran away. It was the first place any of us looked. All I saw were the headstones of the people Llorona said she could hear if she really listened. I prayed Llorona was not with the dead, her voice joining theirs.

I went to the second place I always looked, The Economy.

Benny was behind the counter, his Bible laid out in front of him, opened next to the box of lighters that looked like pistols, the packets of vitamins, the free penny dish, the stink bombs. His mouth was moving, but no sound came out, and he didn't even look up like he usually did.

I whistled through my teeth to get his attention.

Without looking up, he said, "Did you know the Word says that God listens to the prayers of a righteous man? Sometimes I don't feel like a righteous man. I know I am washed clean by the Blood of Jesus, that the things I have done and will do have been thrown into a sea of forgetfulness. I mean I know all that."

I didn't know what to say. I knew what was on his mind, his sobrino in a hospital hurt and put in a place in life that Benny could have been in, a fate he had not saved Smiley from. I had never heard Benny talk like this. He always talked about God, but he never talked about himself that way.

"I have been praying for days, that Ismael would get better and be able to walk and talk again. I have been to the hospital, have anointed his forehead with oil like it says to do in James, but he is not getting better the way I had asked. He doesn't even look at anyone. It's almost like there is no one inside anymore. Why would God allow that? I mean I know He has a purpose for everything and everyone. But mi'jito Smiley never hurt anyone." There were tears pooled in his eyes, and I realized the whole time he had been talking to me, he hadn't even looked up once.

"What do the doctors say?" I asked, even though I didn't want to talk about Smiley. If I talked about him, I would start crying too, and I didn't need that right now.

"You pray and fast, pray and fast and you see miracles happen. You see people wake up from comas. Your jefita gets better from the nerves and the anxiety. Your wife forgives you when she shouldn't anymore. But this one? I haven't seen any healing happen for Ismael, no getting better or even just a little sign of getting better. I know I just have to believe, have faith in the Word, that God hears the prayers of a righteous man, that I am righteous, that all the things I have done have been forgiven."

"Do they say he is going to get better and be like he was?"

"This one time a camarada from church told me that God hears and answers *all* of our prayers, every single one, but that sometimes the answer is no. We have to be okay with whatever He says, even if we don't like it at first. I wonder if the answer is no." I turned to go because I wasn't hearing that.

He walked around the counter and put his hand on my shoulder, looking at me for the first time. "Espérate, I want to tell you something. Whatever happens, mi'jo, I want you to know this. It is God's will, even if I hate it right now. We have to accept it."

He must have seen the question that was in me right then. How could Smiley not ever being the same again be something God wanted?

"Sometimes something bad happening to one person can cause some good in another. Did you know that?"

I knew who he was talking about, and it wasn't me. It was about Llorona, the one who was lost.

"You know who I'm talking about, mi'jo. No te hagas." He tried to smile.

"Did you know she used to come in my store late at night and we would talk?"

I turned my lips upside-down, telling him I didn't care either way. I couldn't talk and didn't want to because I knew I would cry and my voice would shake.

"Si es cierto mi'jo, she would come in and we'd talk and I'd tell her *all* about Jesús and what He did for me when I was in the bote. I told her He was the only one who cared for me and got me the job at the Economy ¿Y sabes qué? Anytimes I said Jesús she would walk out and wave her hand, telling me, 'Te guacho.' She would want to leave kind of like you right now."

This sounded like the Llorona I knew.

"Until this one time the other night I asked her if she knew why La Llorona walks along the river, crying y crying, asking where her babies are. She told me what everybody else thinks, that it's because she feels guilty for drowning her children. I said that wasn't it at all. You shoulda seen how she just looked at me like I was the stupidest dummy she ever knew. Anyway, I said the *real* reason is because La Llorona didn't know nothing about forgiveness. I said she hadn't forgiven herself or the man who hurt her and she hadn't accepted God's forgiveness for *her*. And you know what? She understood this. I told her if La Llorona just did *that* she'd find peace and she wouldn't cry anymore. If she would just forgive herself, accept God's forgiveness, He would give her a new name instead of La Llorona. After I told her all this she started crying for real, mi'jo. I didn't know what to do so I just started praying, but with my eyes open like I was just talking to her and God together so she wouldn't get all scared. And we started praying, and pretty soon she was saying a prayer, where she was asking Jesús to be saved from everything, asking to forgive and to be forgiven, telling Him she believed He died on the cross for her. We said 'amen' together and you should've seen her smile. I *never* saw her smile like that. She didn't even cover her teeth like she does. I told her she had a new name now, one that only *God* knew, and she didn't have to stay in the same place, crying and crying like La Llorona for what she had done. I told her it was time to move on."

"When did this happen?"

"The night after we heard about Ismael."

I was out of the store before he could say anything else, tell me to be careful, or ask God to bless me on my way. I especially did not want him to ask me to pray to accept Jesus, because if he asked me to, I knew I would stop and pray with him, and right now I *had* to leave.

Then I was going further down Bonham closer and closer to her house.

I walked fast past the dog that always barked next door to Llorona's house, the one I could never see through the fence and the bushes, no matter how hard I looked for him.

Her house on Garza Avenue was sad-looking like always, the chipped paint and the windows open, the curtains moving like a woman's hair. There was this pile of ashes on the dry lawn, with pieces of black glass broken everywhere. What could have happened? Only a couple of lights were on, with all those candles turned off. I thought I would try this last place. Try to find Llorona for all of us.

That same smell came out to me through the burglar bars, cooked onions, and clothes that had been sitting in the sun. I knocked on the door.

"¿Quién es?" I heard her mother say.

"Cirilo."

"Ay," she said. "Pásale, pásale." I had not expected this, for her to invite me in so quickly.

The few times I'd actually looked at Llorona's mother from the sidewalk or seen her go to her room whenever I came inside, I'd never seen anything of Llorona's features, not the hair or the face or the same small bones. Llorona's mother had black around her eyes and a mean mouth. Her hair was curly, going everywhere. She scratched her head with those long nails of hers, the ones with painted designs. Her makeup was too white for her so she looked like she was wearing a mask. I sat down and she offered me tea or water. Something inside of me was afraid she would put poison in it that would make me die or sick because maybe she blamed me for Llorona's sadness.

"You know what happened to her?" she said in Spanish.

This was the first time I ever noticed she and Llorona had the same black eyes, with no light passing through.

"No, Señora Galán, I don't know, that's why I came. Do you know where she is?"

"I am not asking you because I want to know. I am asking you to see if you know what happened to her. That girl she was always leaving, but this time, this time she is gone. Pobrecita mi'ja, she is gone forever." It was probably worse than any of us thought.

"So then where did she go?"

"Like I was telling you she was always going, coming in, but not coming home. I just did not know what to do. Going up and going down, coming and leaving, always that way with her." She was crying now, her eyes black and wet with her mascara.

"Where did she go?"

"I cannot believe what she did to me," she said, waving her arms around the room without any candles. "You know I went out in the yard with a Rosary? I held the beads out in front of me, like this, and waited till it started moving from side to side." Señora Galán sat there nodding her head and swaying left to right. "I faced the four directions: East, West, South and when I faced the North, it started to move and then I knew what happened to her. I did not want to believe it, but I knew."

"Where. Did. She. Go."

She kept talking like she hadn't even heard what I'd said. "What is it, why is it that they always leave? Just like her father, always leaving. Even when he was here, he was always going somewhere, his mind walking out the door, going out to find some younger woman, somewhere else he could make another family."

I stood up, threw my hand at her in the way that says, *Que ya, forget about you*, and left her there. She said, "Listen, you and me, we are the same, somebody is always going to leave us and we cannot do anything about it. There are only two kinds of people. Those who leave and those who are abandoned. We are the last kind. We can light a candle to God and when He does not listen we can light one to the devil, but they are not going to help us. You see? In the end, even *they* leave us."

My hand was on the door when she said, "And Karina? She went away. That is all you have to know. If I tell you, if I do what she told me to do in her letter, then she got her way. If you walk out of here right now without walking into her bedroom and finding out what happened, you can leave her and *you* win. You. Leave. Her. You win because you do not care what happened to her. Understand? Not the other way around. If you walk in and find out, she is always going to be leaving you, always going to be out of the touch of your fingers, always disappearing around a corner where you cannot touch her. It is not too late to leave her."

"I need to know," I said and stepped back into the house.

She said, "Then you are going to know and when you see, finally, you are going to know my heart, know what it is to lose."

"Señora Galán, I already know."

"You think you do, but you do not. A boy like you does not know what it is to lose. You still think you will live forever. You think that your body will always be beautiful, that your face will always be that of an angel's. You do not know what comes next. Go into her room and see what she left you."

As I walked away from her towards Llorona's room, I thought maybe Llorona had finally gotten her way, finished what she wanted to do in junior high when she wanted to jump off the stadium, finally did what Charter Palms tried to stop her from doing. I saw her in my mind, all cold and stiff, her black eyes white from death. Me leaning over to kiss Llorona, her blue lips not giving me anything except the understanding of what it was to lose.

Llorona helped me understand in another way.

She was not there.

Instead, she left a piece of herself. There on her bed was the book she wrote her poems in, where she drew her pictures, one of those composition books with the covers that look like empty TV screens when you see the snow, the only snow any of us who stay in the Valley will ever see. The room was like it always was, pictures of me and Llorona and all our friends. She had not taken anything down when we broke up. The picture with us at a party, me holding her, Llorona's arms in front of her, throwing HCP and holding some-body's fake pistol. Dried roses hanging upside down, the ones I had given to her when she turned fifteen and she didn't get a quinceañera because her parents didn't have enough money. The mum I bought her last year for homecoming, with green and silver ribbons, little gold footballs and cheerleader cones tied to ribbons. Llorona didn't wear it that day at school because she said it looked stupid, and we got into this big fight about it. She didn't tell me how much it meant to her, but I knew because all that day she took Brenda and Gladis and all her friends to her locker to show them her mum. I moved one of the ribbons with a bell tied to it, and there wasn't a sound more sad than this.

I sat on the bed and opened the book. I read a few words, wanting real bad to find my name. Then I opened it up to the last couple of pages and I understood.

In these pages of her composition book, Llorona made a picture with words, about what happened the night Smiley got shot, then the night she went away.

The way she explained it, in the early morning before the sun came out, when Smiley was in the hospital, Llorona got out the backpack where she'd packed as many clothes as she could. She had a hundred and eighty-nine dollars and a bus ticket to somewhere she didn't say. Her mother had said that Llorona went north, and all I could think of was that she was going to San Antonio to look for her father, but in all those words written in her composition book, Llorona didn't say *where* she was going, just that she had to go, that there was something important she needed to tell someone. This was the Llorona all of us know, just like the one from the fantasma stories. She only gave us a little of herself, but never enough to solve the mystery of her. You could hear her crying by the river, but never actually see her.

After Llorona got ready to go, while her mother was asleep, she went through all her mother's hechizera tools, the herbs she used in her curses, dried rooster feet, the rotting goat hooves, and the black candles she burned to the devil, her oils and her powders. She put all of these things into grocery bags and took them out to the front yard. Llorona poured lighter fluid on the bags and dropped a match in. A blue fire started, and soon everything was burning. In that morning quietness, Llorona heard whispers coming from the flames.

She wrote, *I did it for love.* She did it so her mother would let go of all that brujería, stop making curses and promises, hoping her man would come home. The stars were fading and soon the sky would go white. She knew that during the day she wouldn't be brave enough to do what she had to, leave her mother like her father had.

On her pillow was a black cross necklace like the ones they made in prison. These prisoners undid black dress socks, or used yarn if they had it, and then tied knots and knots so tight until they started to make a cross. They made them with two colors, one always black and the other, red or blue or maroon, whatever their color was. Some of them left the threads loose at the bottom of the cross or they burned them with matches. This little one I was holding, the one Llorona had made for me some time before she left, was all black, with no other color mixed in.

I kissed the cross Llorona had made and it smelled like her, like the sweetness on her forehead and the back of her neck, as if she'd been wearing it just a couple of seconds before, as if I'd just missed her. I put it on like she asked me to in those last couple of sentences she'd written: *I, Karina, want you to wear this cross, and think of our love. I want you to remember it because it wasn't you I was leaving. It wasn't you, and you didn't do anything wrong.* But it was me, I thought, and all of this was my fault. What Benny hadn't realized when he told her about La Llorona needing forgiveness was that the soldier who could not forgive La Llorona for drowning her children also needed forgiveness. He was the real villain in the story. In this story of La Llorona, I was the children she had drowned, yes, but I was also the soldier, the one who had not forgiven and kept the tragedy in motion. I was the victim and also the villain.

So this was what it was to be abandoned, knowing the only thing in life that will never leave you is pain and sadness that goes down into your bones. Our whole lives we fought against this loneliness, waited and waited for it to pass, to be with someone else who would talk to us in the dark. Like my own 'Buelita Guadalupe rubbing her rosary beads, crossing herself against fears of the night. Pop and Mama drinking in the cantinas just so they wouldn't be in the dark quiet of our house where they felt more alone when it was just them two together. Ángel and Smiley's mother lighting candles at the shrine of her dead husband, praying and praying his pictures could come to life. Ángel using girls for the love they wanted to give him. Smiley making his own world through his drawings, a world that was always good to him, now trapped alone in his mind, not able to talk or look at any of us. All the youngsters everywhere getting initiated so they could say *HCP love* or whatever, as long as they could say the word *love* and feel it was a part of them, and that it meant they were not alone anymore. Señora Galán putting on the magical Return to Me powder after she took her baths, repeating her husband's name like a prayer so he'd come home. And us, me and Karina, kissing, sharing those beautiful seconds we knew we'd lose. All of this to fight being alone, to pass the hours until we could find others as lonely as us.

Her mother was wrong, and Benny had to be right. Sometimes you had to have the bad before the good. Sometimes people left just so they could come back and be new, be someone they never were. Until I saw her again I'd hold onto these two pieces of Karina: her book and our cross without Jesús on it. The last she had written was this: *Jesús is not on the cross you see because He has gone onto something better. He had to go even though He knew people would be sad with His disappearance. In His leaving people had to finally understand who He was. When He was buried, and He came back to life, Jesús left the cloth He was buried in, to tell them He would be back. I leave these promesas to tell you the same. Mi querido, mi oración, mi Cirilo.* Each page, each poem she wrote was a message telling me that *this girl with the new name* would come back when she was ready, that I was supposed to hold these promises for her until she did. And if anybody asked I would say the cross around my neck wasn't made by some prisionera, but by a spirit who was once named Llorona, a girl with a new name who was now free, away from all this.

EPILOGUE

BEFORE ÁNGEL, SMILEY, AND Llorona were in my life, and when my parents were happier and not drinking so much, Sundays meant church and Papa Tavo and 'Buelita Guadalupe's house. Now, in the middle of my junior year of life, Sundays meant driving to my grandparents' house without my parents. Pop had bought me an emerald green '69 Impala he'd bought at an auction in San Antonio. It had a clean body, but needed some work. He said that I would need to get a job soon to make payments to him, and the only reason he had gotten it for me at all was because I needed to drive myself around, but I knew he was just trying to bribe me into not complaining about having to go to a new school. Smiley and Ángel would have loved it, and would have helped me trick it out.

After everything went down with Ángel and Smiley, Pop had moved me to Sharyland High School for my junior and senior year, saying I needed to get away from those vagos and make some new friends, which I really hadn't. The only one I knew at school at all was Bell. So now my Sundays weren't about Westside Park, but all about having lunch with 'Buelita: her guisos, mole, or chicken and rice, and always her tortillas. Other times there were pachangas, parties for my little cousins' birthdays, or get-togethers just because. Ever since my grandfather Papa Tavo had had a nervous breakdown and was placed in the nursing home at the San Juan Shrine, Sundays also meant going there too. It was a way to not be alone, but also a way for me to remember how it was before everything had happened, before I lost the only friends I'd ever really known.

This one Sunday, I especially wanted to go to 'Buelita's because my cousin Erika, tía Marisol and tío Lalo's daughter, was having her third birthday party. Almost all of the Izquierdos were going to be there. Even a few of my tíos and tías had come down from San Antonio for the weekend. My little cousin Erika was something else. At two, she had attitude walking around with a toy purse and telling us 'no' any time we tried to hug her or get some kisses. She also danced like Selena any time one of her songs came on the radio or her dad asked her to show how she danced at our tía Suzana's wedding.

'Buelita's neighborhood, La Zavala in McAllen, wasn't East Los, and the Zavaleros wouldn't blast you if they didn't know you, but the locos still looked at you gacho if you didn't belong or they had never seen your car before. The only times they'd mess you up is if you came in throwing colors or signs, just asking for trouble like some junior high wannabe. This was my father's barrio, where he used to run around with his brothers, causing panic around town, when he was in Los Diggers.

Me, they knew I was all Dennett, but they also knew who my Pop was and that I was an Izquierdo and that I had been coming there since I was a kid. We'd all seen each other since we were little, me and my cousins walking to the corner store or to play on the swings behind St. Joseph's church. I'd even played football with some of them way back then. So I'd drive up Ithaca Avenue in my old-new Impala and none of them threw me even a sideways glance. Only the younger ones without respect, little junior high punks trying to act all bad, stared me down as if it would scare me. I had to laugh. They had no way of knowing the things I had seen, the things I had done.

As soon as I rolled up, I could smell the smoke from the barbecue pit. With this smell of mesquite and fajitas, with the sounds of my tíos laughing, with my tías talking inside beyond the burglar bars, with my little cousins running around my legs, I almost forgot everything that had happened in my life, who I had lost. Then, I thought of my Papa Tavo, how he was sick in the nursing home and would not last much longer and knew I had to stop feeling sorry for myself.

People all over the Zavala could smell that barbecue chicken and those fajitas coming from 'Buelita Guadalupe's yard and now everyone inside their houses all around the Zavala wanted to cook-out. Ruben's Grocery would be getting some good business soon. Smelling the fajitas and seeing the smiling faces of my family, I knew I should have started coming around sooner. I could make excuses and say it was because Mama was mad at 'Buelita and not talking to her again or that I had been too busy with my own life, but these were not excuses. These were failings. Even running around wild, I could have made the time. Ángel and Smiley had made time for their mother on Sunday nights. I could have done the same.

When I walked in to 'Buelita's little house, everybody said, "¡Mira, Cirilo!" Most everyone was so excited I was there because me, Pop, and Mama hadn't been to 'Buelita's together in several months. They were glad I was representing my family because this was important, to have at least one person from every family come to the get-togethers or parties. The last time my parents had gone together, 'Buelita had again told Pop and Mama they were spending too much time in the bars, not visiting Papa Tavo my grandfather in the nursing home, and not taking care of me like they were supposed to. 'Buelita had said, *Maybe Cirilo wouldn't have gotten into all of that if you had paid more attention to him. You could have lost him all because you two are so lost in yourselves.* You couldn't tell Mama something like that to her face and have her take it. Once you told her anything or did her wrong, forget it. She would never let it go. Even if she did talk nice to you afterward, this thing would always be there, behind her eyes, in the way she said things to you. If you said them behind her back, maybe she could ignore it, but this, those words to her face? It would be years before she came around again. And this time my Pop stood by her and hadn't come around either.

My parents hadn't spoken to 'Buelita since that argument, but they didn't care if I went to her house. This silence between them was not just because of the argument, even if that's what Mama said. It had been building for years. They'd never gotten along. Before they got married, Pop messed up by telling Mama what 'Buelita had told him about her. *That woman, she is going to be very expensive,* 'Buelita had said. Mama had never really forgiven 'Buelita for saying that. With the way Mama bought gold jewelry all the time, and had her hair done by her hairdresser for seventy or eighty dollars, and her nails done downtown, 'Buelita had pretty much been right. Anyway, if my parents ever got mad that I was here at 'Buelita's, I'd still go. They couldn't stop me.

I went into the kitchen, which was elbow to elbow full of my tíos. They were cutting more fajitas, laughing with pink meat and fat in their hands. The Three Amigos Gordos everyone called my uncles Lalo, Manuel, and Joe because of their beer bellies. They held out the meat in front of my face. My tío Manuel gave me his elbow to shake since his hands were full. My tío Lalo laughed his big belly laugh, said, "Good to see you, mi'jo!" and patted me on the back in his rough way. When I was smaller and he used to do this, it almost knocked me down. Now, at seventeen, I could stand up without losing my balance. I was getting taller than all of my uncles, even though everyone said I was so skinny I looked like a stick standing next to them.

Tío Gonzalo shook my hand, smiled, and took a plate of raw, seasoned chicken out to the barbecue pit.

My tías were all sitting at the table, drinking wine coolers and some drinking coffee, even though it was so hot, especially in the kitchen where there was the pot of charro beans on the stove.

I bent and kissed my aunts on the cheeks, one by one. When I got to tía Marisol, I said, "Tía, are you losing weight?" I said this every time I saw her, but it was never true. She was good to me, and it made her feel better. Any time she saw me, she didn't say things like *Long time no see stranger* or *Where have you been?* or ask about my parents. She didn't judge or give me the evil eye because of what my parents had done. My tía Marisol was just happy to see me.

"Ay, mi'jo, gracias for noticing. I'm on the low-carb diet where I can eat a lot of meat and bacon and barbacoa, but no bread or tortillas. Why don't you tell your tío I've lost weight, mi'jo? He don't seem to notice." She said this last part, pointing her eyebrows at tío Lalo who was chopping at the chicken, cutting it down the middle and laughing the whole time.

I winked at my tía and said, "Oye, tío have you noticed my tía's losing weight? She's looking fine. You better watch out the next time you go to a dance." All my tías laughed and tía Marisol said, "*Ay, mi'jo*, you're crazy."

Tío Lalo lifted his shirt and patted his own big, hairy stomach. "Hey, vieja, look right here. Mira. You know what? You can never leave my beauty. I got you under my power."

"Power, ni que power," my aunt said, rolling her eyes.

I looked around for 'Buelita, but I was sure she wasn't in the room since tío Lalo would never do anything like that in front of her. He loved and respected 'Buelita, his mother-in-law, as much as his own mother. I also looked around for my tía Victoria, my uncle Gonzalo's new, younger wife. If Ángel or Smiley saw her, they would say she was *bien* buena. I heard Smiley's voice in my head saying it, a voice I would never hear again. I started to think of the brothers, then changed my thoughts to something else, which is something I had been doing a lot lately. Anyway, my aunt was another reason I liked to come around. Who doesn't like to talk to a pretty woman? At twenty-seven and as good-looking as she was, she could have gone cruising with us and no one would have thought anything about it except that we'd done good for ourselves.

"Where's 'Buelita?" I said.

"She's in Suzana's room. Go say hi, mi'jo, she'll be happy to know you're here."

When my tía Suzana got married to this little Mexican national named Artemio who used to be a horse jockey, she moved out of her room at 'Buelita's. Then, 'Buelita turned Suzana's room into a place to pray, like a mini-version of the San Juan del Valle Shrine. This was around the same time Papa Tavo went into Charter Palms for getting agitated whenever there was a full moon. With my grandfather out in the yard looking for buried black magic curses and yelling at the top of his lungs in the middle of the night, what else could she do but say it was okay to put him there and pray and pray that he would get better?

After Charter Palms, his liver got sick from all the nervous anxiety medicine he was taking. Then, he moved from nursing home to nursing home, to the place where he was now, San Juan Nursing Home at the San Juan Shrine. 'Buelita prayed for Papa Tavo, but she also prayed because she was afraid. She would call my pop before when they were still talking, or now she called my tío Gonzalo or Lalo in the middle of the night so they could come check around the house. She said bad kids in the neighborhood were always crossing through her yard, looking into windows for something they could steal. Whenever Pop or one of my tíos got there, they never saw anything, any gangsters, or any sign the gangsters had been there. This was also another reason why Mama didn't like 'Buelita. She thought 'Buelita did it for attention.

There was a little black and white TV screen in the living room. It had four different pictures, and as I looked closer, it was four different angles of her yard.

"Po'recita," I said to myself. The TV screen was hooked up to surveillance cameras tío Gonzalo had installed outside. I imagined 'Buelita sitting there at night, next to the phone, just waiting to see some kids jump the fence. I mean what kind of barrio was it where kids from the neighborhood were trying to steal things from an old woman in the *same* neighborhood? Messed *up*. It was never supposed to be this way, even though I'm sure it also happened in Dennett.

I heard her whispered prayers. Her prayer voice made me calm like it did during all those Christmases when she prayed the rosary and all I could think about was opening presents.

Her back was to me and she was kneeling down. She could stay that way longer than anyone I'd seen. I knew this because some Christmases we'd say the rosary inside, on our knees. Us kids shifted from knee to knee because it hurt us so much, but 'Buelita would be there, not moving at all, her eyes shut tight, her spirit somewhere far away from us, whispering every bead. Once, inside the church at San Juan, after all of us had visited Papa Tavo, she had walked on her knees all the way from the back to the altar in the front. All the way, on her knees.

At the top of her altar was a framed picture of the Virgen de Guadalupe, the one that you see on Rollin' Low T-shirts and lowriders, the one where she's wearing the blue cape with twelve stars on it and the half-moon under her brown feet. 'Buelita also had this big wooden rosary hanging, the crucifix as big as a hammer, the beads as big as pecans. There was also this picture of Jesus hanging where if you looked at it from one side, he was kneeling by some rock and if you looked at it another way, he was bleeding, with his sad crying eyes looking up to the Father who knew this was the way it had to be. I used to draw this face all the time and had even won an art award my freshman year. The drawing I had done was on the wall next to that picture I had copied, along with some of my other cousins' drawings and essays from school.

I stood there by the open door, watching her, noticing how her ponytail had gotten more white hair in it. I didn't say anything.

"Come in, mi'jo," she said without turning. In Spanish, she said, "I want to talk to you."

"How did you know it was me? Did God tell you I would come?"

"No, mi'jo, I heard everyone when they said, '¡Mira Cirilo!' Also, I heard you driving your old car."

She stayed on her knees for a little too long, like she wanted me to get down on the floor with her too. I stayed standing by the door because I wasn't ready for that.

I felt better when she motioned for me to help her get up. 'Buelita held out her arms. I gave her my abrazo, the kind of tight hug I saved for my grandmother, and inhaled lavender and lotion, the clean beautiful smell of my 'Buelita. In Spanish, she said, "How are you this week, m'ijo?"

"Sí, 'Buelita, I've been good this week."

We were still hugging each other when she said, "Qué bueno, qué bueno. It is always so good to see you, to hear you are doing better and that you are okay," sounding like she was about to cry. I was glad when she didn't. I could stand to hear anyone else but my grandmother cry, even Mama.

"What I wanted to tell you was I have been praying for you and your father and mother, and I know it is all going to get better. God told me your father is going to change."

What about my mother? I thought, but didn't ask. I just said, "That's good, 'Buelita, that's good."

"No, mi'jo, I know it is good, but you have to believe it. And I am not saying this to make you feel better. I am saying this because I know. But your mother? I do not know."

After a couple hours, when more people showed up, like tía Victoria and Little Gonzalo, they decided to put up the piñata. Because I was pretty skinny and didn't weigh that much and was old enough to go on the roof, they asked me to control the piñata, a clown with a big balloon stomach, the big kind you bought in Reynosa and not one of those cheap little ones from the Central. This was going to be fun, being on the other side of the piñata for once, doing the job of an uncle, being the one teasing the little kids.

All my little cousins had tried to bust the piñata already. I had been good to them, but sometimes piñatas were very thick, and no matter how hard they swung the broomstick, the little kids couldn't bust it.

My cousin Seferino, the oldest kid there, was up to bat last, and since he was big enough, he had a blindfold on. Sef looked like a little tío Lalo with those small eyes and that big stomach. He spit on his hands, rubbed them together, and said, "Bring it on, cachetón!" Sef swung the broomstick wild and I pulled on the piñata. It went rolling through the air, and everyone went, "Oh!" He was swinging wild, not even coming close, and everybody kept moving out more and more because he had a lot of weight behind his swing. Somebody could get hurt.

When Sef stopped, I put the piñata on top of his head and lifted the clown as soon as he tried to hit it.

Sef said, "*Ya güey*, don't be like that."

Tío Lalo said, "Sef," because he'd said 'güey' in front of 'Buelita. It was okay for Sef to say it in front of him, just not in front of 'Buelita, even though *güey* wasn't that bad of a word. It was like saying *man* or *dude*, but it was a respect thing not saying it in front of people older than you.

Finally, because I could tell everyone was getting bored, thinking, *Ya, let him hit it already, our kids want some candy!* I kept it from moving, and Sef took this big swing. Candy went flying everywhere, but Sef kept going.

All the grownups said, "Wait, wait, *wait!*" but Sef kept on anyway, and Little Gonzalo ran in. You see, when you're hitting a piñata or standing around the circle waiting for candy, something takes over you. You can't hear what the grownups are saying. All you're thinking about is busting that piñata way open or running and grabbing as much candy as you can. It's like when somebody's getting jumped, and nobody wants to stop, even when the teachers and chotas finally show up, break through the crowd, and are yelling and pulling you off of each other. It was like so many fights I had seen or been in.

I was above everybody, and I saw it happen all slow-motion before everyone else. The broomstick came back as Sef was going for another swing and—*Zas!*—my cousin Little Gonzalo's head was there. He was on the ground now and stupid Sef, all crazy with thoughts of candy, couldn't hear all the grownups saying, "Stop! *Stop* it!" Finally, he stopped because my tío Lalo slapped him on the back of the head. Tía Victoria went to Little Gonzalo. All the kids didn't care. They were stepping over Little Gonzalo, making candy bags out of their shirts, holding them out with one hand and throwing candy in with the other.

Tía Victoria was sitting there, and she wasn't over-reacting and treating Little Gonzalo like a baby, even though he was screaming and rolling around in the dirt. She was saying, "It's okay, mi'jo, you're all right. You don't need to cry." His head was going to have this big chipote, a big bump, but there wasn't any blood. Little Gonzalo just kept sucking in air and trying to bury his face into tía Victoria, saying, "Mama, Mama, Mama." When I saw her face, and her eyes were looking into mine, I felt bad about making Seferino have to work at hitting the piñata. Maybe if I'd made it easier, Seferino wouldn't have gone so crazy with the stick. She smiled at me and shook her head as if to say everything was okay.

Tía said, "Sana, sana, colita de rana, si no sanarás, sanarás, mañana." Our mothers say this when we're hurt, but not too bad. It means, *Heal, heal, little frog's tail. If you don't heal today, you'll heal tomorrow.* It doesn't sound the same in English though. Little Gonzalo would not get up or look at any of us. Like I thought, there was this big red chipote on his forehead, like this big avocado pit was growing inside, but he was going to be okay, if he ever stopped crying.

Tía Victoria said, "Go play, mi'jo, go play. You're all right. Be a tough little man." She wasn't treating him like that because she didn't care about him, but because she didn't want him to be a mama's boy. Everybody knows mama's boys get jumped, so it was a good thing she didn't baby him. I hoped Little Gonzalo got over this before he went to school, because the first time he did this at school, it would be all over for him. The other kids would knock him down just to watch the show.

Sef went up to Little Gonzalo with his shirt full of candy, his big panza showing to everybody, and told him he was sorry. "You want to share my candy?"

Now, we were all sitting down at the table in the kitchen eating. The little kids were in the living room watching a cartoon video someone had put on. We were eating serious, no talking at all. You could hear the sound of ice in our glasses of Coke, the sound of our arms sticking to the plastic cover on the table. Once in a while, someone would ask if there were more tortillas and someone would get up to heat more.

I was sitting next to tía Victoria, and Little Gonzalo was on her lap holding a bag of ice to his forehead. This was the way they were, always talking to each other real quiet, like they were telling secrets, always praying together before they ate. They were *Hallelujahs* and Victoria was known for busting out in tongues in church or whenever we prayed as a family, while Little Gonzalo could supposedly translate everything she said. Some of my older cousins like Sef sometimes made fun of Little Gonzalo, saying, *Hey translate this, primo!* and then say some maldiciones. This would make Little Gonzalo run and cry, but I always stuck up for him. If they messed with him, I gave them nacas, the thing I did where I got them in a headlock and hit the tops of their heads with my middle knuckle.

"So, what's up, LG?" I said. "You break any hearts at the preschool yet?"

Little Gonzalo smiled real big, and lowered the bag of ice he held on his forehead.

"Ay, Cirilo," tía Victoria said, and put the ice pack back on the chipote. "Don't encourage him. That boy is puro Izquierdo." She meant that all us boys and men with Izquierdo blood were dogs. We could always get pretty women without even trying too hard.

"Do you know what they caught him doing at daycare?"

"Oh no, tía, what? Being travieso?"

"Much worse. They found him and this little girl hiding in the gabinetes underneath the sink. I said, 'Mi'jo, your daycare's called

Little Friends, not Little Kissy Friends. So don't be kissing girls in any cabinets!' This one's going to be bad. Va ser terrible."

Little Gonzalo smiled bigger at the word *terrible*.

"Little man knows. Ain't that right, LG?"

"I like girls," Little Gonzalo said, lifting his shoulders and smiling.

"I know you do, mi'jo. Just like your father and your uncles and your cousin, Cirilo. Y tú, Light Eyes? Got any girlfriends?"

Even before she finished her sentence, I thought of Karina, my Llorona who had gotten away, leaving me here to wait for her, to look for her around every corner, to walk to the mailbox hoping to see one of her illustrated letters or poems.

Tía Victoria didn't need to know about her. "No tía, I don't."

"¿Y porqué no? How can that be?"

"Better being alone. I can go out with my friends without some girl telling me what to do."

"And school, how is school?"

"I'm behind in credits, especially in English."

"Are you going to graduate on time?"

"I hope so. My English teacher told me that I can do a five-page book report or a personal narrative for extra credit and I should be okay and not have to go to summer school again."

"You're smart, m'ijo, you just have to apply yourself."

I smiled and something on my face made her say, "I sounded like an old lady just then didn't I? Like some guidance counselor who's run out of things to say."

"A little bit, tía, but it's okay." She laughed and shook her head. Tío was lucky to have her.

Tía Victoria looked around the table, around the room. Everyone had left. It was just me and her still eating now.

"¿Sabes qué, mi'jo? I'm going to tell you something. And if I sound like a counselor who should retire, I'm sorry. But it needs to be said. Those colored eyes of yours, some girl's going to look into them and see there's something special about you. I go to the mall and to Peter Piper Pizza, and I see all these little gangsters, and in a way, they look just like you with the shaved heads and the baggy clothes. You know those Hispanics who are causing panic. But, you don't want that life. I see something better for you."

"You think so, huh?"

"No, mi'jo, I *know* so. I know you've probably heard it all before, but listen. Tus ojos borrados, those eyes of yours see things others don't. Why do you think you can draw and tell stories so good? It's not in the hands. It's in the eyes. You really look deep into things, see how beautiful they are. Like that one picture of Jesus you drew where He is praying at Gethsemane. You really captured the strength in His face, in His eyes. No wonder you got that award. Mi'jo, just keep it up. Te avientas! You really throw at everything you do! Así, with your art and your words, you just have to share what you've seen, tell everybody what you know."

Afterward, as people were leaving, I drove over to San Juan Nursing Home because I was supposed to meet Pop to visit Papa Tavo.

I walked into the yellow halls and the smell was ugly. This old lady named Margarita was sitting by the TV on her big rolling recliner. She was banging the tray like I'd seen her do every time I'd ever visited. If you didn't see Margarita, you could always *hear* her somewhere, knocking the tray with her fists three times, then clapping three times. She'd sit there, her toothless mouth, her empty eyes looking up into space: knock, knock, knock, clap, clap, clap. Every time. If I ever came in and Margarita wasn't doing it, it'd be because she was gone.

I never liked going to the San Juan Nursing Home, but went anyway, out of respect and love for my grandfather, Papa Tavo. All the older people who went, my tías and tíos, made their kids go. Most of the little ones didn't want to be there because the only Papa Tavo they knew was this sick old man in a nursing home, the one who only talked to us sometimes when he was having a good day.

Other days, Papa Tavo didn't even know who we were, or he just asked us for cigarettes we couldn't give him.

Pop was sitting by the bed, combing Papa Tavo's hair, doing it real slow making sure not to scratch his head. Even though Papa Tavo's mind and body were dying day by day, he had this real long, gray greña that kept growing long no matter what. Why didn't anyone at the nursing home ever comb his hair? His fingernails were the same way, growing and growing and growing.

The Papa Tavo laying there—his thick fingernails like wood, his mouth open, his eyes staring out the window, his skin loose like a paper bag, him not saying much of anything we could understand anymore—was the only grandfather my little cousins had ever known. It was too sad for them because they didn't know him like us older cousins did.

They couldn't remember him going downtown on 17th Street to play dominoes, how he would buy us something from the ice cream truck whenever it came by: ice cream sandwiches, push-ups, or drumsticks. They couldn't know Papa Tavo at the kitchen table, showing me and Sef and my cousin, Dianira, how to play dominoes, ice cream dripping all over the pieces and Papa Tavo not even caring, just laughing with us. The only way they could know this Papa Tavo was from pictures, the grandpa that danced cumbias with 'Buelita at weddings and quinceañeras, his Stetson hat tilted at a cocky angle, back when he still had muscles on him.

Now I got near the bed and Pop said, "Mira, 'Apá, Cirilo. My son is here."

Papa Tavo looked at me without any kind of understanding of who I was.

"Es mi hijo, Cirilo," Pop yelled. "Tu nieto." He didn't seem to understand I was Pop's son or that I was his grandson. He just stared at the ceiling with his mouth open.

I reached out to shake his hand, and he didn't move at all. I took his hand anyway. It was bigger than mine and cold. Sus manos. These hands that had hung drywall and painted houses. These hands that built houses and had rubbed Vicks on my chest when I was a little kid and sick. These hands that had shuffled dominoes.

Just then, Gonzalo, Victoria, and Little Gonzalo walked into the room.

Pop and tío Gonzalo barely gave each other saludos, just a little lifting of the eyebrows and that was it. Pop pretended to wipe some spit away from Papa Tavo's face. Tío Gonzalo was still mad at Pop for the way he was acting with 'Buelita. I didn't blame him, even though brothers were not supposed to act this way.

Tía Victoria said, "¿Y cómo están todos?" Asking us how we were all doing, as if no one was mad.

"We're good. Busy with everything, you know how it is."

She said, "Ay, tell me about it."

You could feel things change between Pop and tío Gonzalo, and they gave each other this nod viejos give, one mixed with respect and regret and a looking forward to a time when things will be different. She told me, "Long time no see, stranger," and we laughed. It was great how women could do this, make things better just by being there.

Tío told Little Gonzalo to go give Papa Tavo his saludo. "Saludale, mi'jo. Go say hi to your grandfather."

Little Gonzalo reached forward and picked up Papa Tavo's hand, not scared like my other little cousins were, who acted bored to try and hide it, and then not even walk into Papa Tavo's room. Tía Victoria was a home health nurse and she sometimes took Little Gonzalo on her visits because the old people liked him. He was never scared of them like most kids so they would always ask tía Victoria about him and give him little strawberry candies whenever he came by. I didn't know if he wasn't scared because he had seen so many old people sick in their beds or because that was just the way he was. Little Gonzalo turned Papa Tavo's hand over and over, and looked at all the wrinkles, the bruised veins and the brown liver spots. He said, "'Buelito, what's all this?"

We all kind of laughed at how Little Gonzalo didn't care what he said, at how he was the only one who talked to Papa Tavo that way. I thought all that about him being a chillón mama's boy didn't matter because Little Gonzalo was brave in his own way, in a way none of the rest of us were or ever would be.

It was quiet and none of us knew what to say. Then, after a little while, Papa Tavo looked down at Little Gonzalo and he actually smiled. I couldn't understand him real good because whenever he did talk it sounded like he was half-asleep, like he had glass marbles in his mouth or something. It sounded like he said, "Esto, mi nieto, es un mapa donde he andado, donde he vivido."

This, my grandson, is a map of where I have been, a map of where I have lived. I looked down, and I knew what he meant about his hands. On his hands, I could read where Papa Tavo had been: the large spots were places he had stayed, the smaller ones the places he had visited, every wrinkle a dusty sendero he had taken to get him here across the river, every vein a street he had used to get him to work, the clear spaces in between where he had never been and never would go.

I turned my own hands over and held them out. The map was mostly clear with large open spaces I would claim for the Izquierdos, clear with undiscovered trails and roads I would map out for Papa Tavo and the rest of us. Along the way, I would meet others and tell them about what I had seen and what I knew. I would begin by telling them about the summer between the sophomore and junior years of my life, starting my personal narrative, my story with me sitting on the porch waiting for Ángel and Smiley, thinking about what it meant to be alone. Then I would tell them the rest, about how even when you are alone or lose someone, you can find hope, even if it is in the smallest of things: a tiny black cross, a book of poems, a goodbye that might not really be a goodbye from a girl who taught you how to love.

CPSIA information can be obtained
at www.ICGtesting.com
Printed in the USA
LVHW111437110619
620862LV00005B/53/P

9 781532 665073